Chase Baker and the Golden Condor

(A Chase Baker Thriller #2)

Vincent Zandri

PRAISE FOR VINCENT ZANDRI

Scream Catcher

"Sensational . . . masterful . . . brilliant."
—*New York Post*

"My fear level rose with this Zandri novel like it hasn't done before. Wondering what the killer had in store for Jude and seeing the ending, well, this is one book that will be with me for a long time to come!"
—Reviews by Molly

"I very highly recommend this book . . . It's a great crime drama that is full of action and intense suspense, along with some great twists . . . Vincent Zandri has become a huge name and just keeps pouring out one best seller after another."
—Life in Review

"A thriller that has depth and substance, wickedness and compassion."
—*The Times-Union* (Albany)

"I also sat on the edge of my seat reading about Jude trying to stay alive when he was thrown into one of those games . . . Add to that having to disarm a bomb for good measure!"
—Telly Says

Lost Grace

"Lost Grace is a gripping psychological thriller that will keep you riveted on the edge of your seat as you turn the pages."
—Jersey Girl Book Reviews

"This book is truly haunting and will stay with you long after you have closed the covers."
—Beth C., Amazon 5-star review

The Innocent

"The action never wanes."
—*Fort Lauderdale Sun-Sentinal*

"Gritty, fast-paced, lyrical and haunting."
—Harlan Coben, bestselling author of *Six Years*

"Tough, stylish, heartbreaking."
—Don Winslow, bestselling author of *Savages*

ALSO BY VINCENT ZANDRI

The Dick Moonlight Mystery Series

Moonlight Falls
Moonlight Mafia
Moonlight Rises
Blue Moonlight
Full Moonlight
Murder by Moonlight

The Jack Marconi Mystery Series

The Innocent
Godchild
The Guilty

The Chase Baker Action/Adventure Series

The Shroud Key

The Stand-Alones

Everything Burns
The Remains
Scream Catcher
Lost Grace
The Concrete Pearl
Permanence

The Shorts

Pathological
Banal
True Stories

First Edition ~ November 2014
Vincent Zandri © copyright 2014

Bear Media
4 Orchard Grove, Albany, NY 12204
http://www.vincentzandri.com

Author Photo by Jessica Painter

Published in the United States of America

"The Ancient Astronauts or ancient aliens' theory is a pseudo-scientific proposal that posits intelligent extraterrestrial beings have visited Earth and made contact with humans in antiquity and prehistory. Proponents suggest that this contact influenced the development of human cultures, technologies, and religions."
—*Wikipedia*

"The Amazon Rainforest is so large, in fact, that there are still tribes of people untouched by modern civilization. The Amazon maintains perhaps the most species rich tract of tropical rainforest on the planet. It is beautiful to behold, but dangerous in traveling. Dense bush and a slew of venomous creatures keep the common person from delving too deep."
— *Smashing Lists: Top 10 Least Explored Places in the World*

PROLOGUE

Machu Picchu
Urubamba Valley
Amazon Basin (Amazonia), Peru
May 1939

Yanking back his goggles and *resting them on the brim of his pilot's cap, Peter C. Keogh reaches into his waist-length leather pilot's coat and pulls out his map. His thighs pressed together in order to hold the stick steady, the forty-year-old freelance employee of Standard Oil exhales.*

A sea of green stretches for as far as the eyes can see. A forest-covered jagged mountain landscape that is as unrelenting in its thickness as it is in its sheer vastness. The retired US Army Colonel turned explorer-for-hire pulls back on the throttle of his de Havilland DH 82 Tiger Moth and begins to descend toward the tree-topped canopy of a valley split in two by the white-capped waters of the fast-moving Urubamba River. Wiping away some of the condensate from his goggle lenses with the tips of his leather-gloved fingers, he leans his head out over the fuselage to get a better bird's-eye view of the territory below.

"You've got to be here somewhere, you snake," he speaks into the cool, humid wind that slaps his face as he searches for an elusive break in a jungle that blankets the back half of Machu Picchu and beyond.

The unexplored half.

While his blue, eagle-like eyes search, his brain pictures the five-thousand-dollar bonus waiting for him. The cash comes to him only if he can locate a trail extension the famous cartographer and explorer Dr. Hiram Bingham described in eloquent prose more than twenty years ago—a trail that begins at the backside of Machu Picchu and ends at the mouth of the Amazon River inside the Amazon basin at a place untouched by the modern world, a place known only as Inferno.

1

He opens the map just enough so that it doesn't blow away in the gale force winds. Looking up quickly at the brown, barren, boulder-strewn summit of Machu Picchu in the distance, he then looks back down upon the map.

"The Machu Picchu summit is my benchmark which means you must be directly below me. But where?"

Folding the map back up and stuffing it back into his coat pocket, he reaches down to the floor with his free hand and grabs hold of his 16mm Eyemo movie camera, the same make and model his young friend Bob Capa used recently in and around the bombed out streets of civil war–plagued Spain. Leaning the lens over the side, Keogh presses the trigger on the camera and starts shooting footage regardless of the fact that the trail he's being paid to "rediscover" is nowhere to be seen.

"This is all because of you, Hiram, baby," Keogh whispers to himself, his words fading into the wind. "I don't come back with proof of a trail, I not only don't get my bonus, the bastards will make me return my entire advance. And now that I'm a dad, I need the dough. Just need to get a little lower ..."

Luckily, Keogh knows that movie cameras—even the super-high-tech hand-held ones like the Eyemo—often pick up details that the naked eye cannot see, and that's what he's banking on right at this moment. That the camera lens will somehow break through the dense foliage and capture, even if only for a fleeting second, a humble visual hint of trailhead made of dirt or stone that will lead Standard Oil to believe they can guide a team of drillers into the Amazon basin in order to mine its vast resources of black gold. Fact is, Keogh is counting on it.

But what he's not counting on is what can go wrong when he takes his eyes off of the horizon for too long. An Army ground commander for most of his adult life, Keogh didn't take to the skies until after his retirement at age thirty-five. Fearless in demeanor and often reckless in flight, his sky instructors would often scold him for "not keeping your goddamned eyes on the road." "What road?" would be the likeable Keogh's common response. A response that would be accompanied by brilliant blue eyes and a smile full of straight white teeth.

That recklessness would prove to be bad luck over the jungle today, as the wheels on the dangerously low-flying Tiger Moth suddenly clip the top of an ironwood tree, causing the nose of the biplane to dip just enough for the propeller to catch a branch. The prop snaps in two. An alarmed Keogh pulls the camera back into the cockpit, drops it onto the floor, and shoves it under the seat. He grabs hold of the joystick, yanks it all the way back in order to gain altitude. But with the prop broken, all he can manage is to make the plane climb a dozen hopeless vertical feet before it stalls, dropping nose first into the thick tree-covered jungle canopy.

***

When Keogh comes to hours later, he finds himself being pulled out of the cockpit of a plane that's snagged itself in the tree branches like a wood and paper kite that's snapped free of its string in a hard wind. The plane's wings have sheared off and the fuselage has capsized, so that if it weren't for the seat belt, Keogh would have surely plunged to the ground one hundred feet below and broken his neck.

Reaching under the seat he grabs hold of the movie camera, holds it tightly while trying his best to maintain consciousness as he eyes the native men who are performing a rescue. Aside from dark leather thongs and sparse ornamentation such as bracelets and necklaces of beads and bones, the short, thickly black-haired, tattooed natives are naked and barefoot. But they work in unison, chanting indiscernible words to unrecognizable tribal tunes as they unbuckle the beat-up pilot from the cockpit seat, carry him down from the trees and then across the jungle floor. Even in his semi-conscious state, and with sharp pain coming from his legs, he senses that the natives don't mean him any harm. But he also knows that their sentiments could change at any moment. The tribes of this jungle are renowned for their head-hunting practices and cannibalism, and should they find his wavy blond-haired, blue-eyed head an attractive sacrifice to the Gods, they won't hesitate to behead him and give over both his heart and entire blood supply to their deities.

Pressing his left bicep against his rib cage, he feels the hard cylinder on his shoulder-holstered Army issue Colt .38 and he feels a sense of profound relief. These natives may indeed try to kill him, but should that happen, he's prepared to take a few of them with him.

As the journey proceeds into the heart of the jungle darkness, Keogh feels the sharp pain in his legs and the sickening dizziness in his head, and passes out again.

The next time he regains consciousness, Keogh finds himself once more gaining altitude. But this time he's not strapped into the cockpit of his Tiger Moth. Instead, the natives are carrying him up a steep set of stairs carved out of the bedrock that constitutes a giant cliff-face. He lies back on a crude gurney made of thick tree branches, animal hide, and rope, and despite the constant sharp pangs of pain, he marvels at his body's ability to remain stuck to it even while being tipped upright, booted feet first, at a severe angle. He's even more impressed with the engineering that had to be involved in carving the staircase from out of this cliff. The team of scantily clad natives might be primitive in appearance and means, but they possess some serious construction skills.

As they climb higher and higher, Keogh begins to notice that the pain coming from his legs is growing progressively worse. Looking down at his lower extremities, he can see the familiar knee-high, lace-up boots, but he also notices something else that stains his canvas trousers.

Blood.

It's then he realizes that both his legs are not only broken, but they are broken badly from compound fractures.

"Gangrene," he whispers to himself. "You can't be far away from me now."

Lying back on the gurney, he pulls a cigar from his coat pocket, along with his lighter, and he fires it up.

Inhaling deeply of the smoke, he silently prays, "My dear Lord, how will I ever get out of here now? I have no plane, no method of communication with the outside world, no legs to walk on. As time goes on, and I do not report in, my employers will assume the worst. That I am dead. They will close the file on me and that will be that. No rescue parties. That was a part of the agreement. The risks I took in taking on this mission were mine alone to assume, and no one else's. I was to either succeed at my mission or fail.

No middle ground. And dear God, have I ever failed. I know it's been a long time since my last confession. Decades, in fact, but please have mercy on my soul. That is, if I've still got one."

The gurney dips and bucks, sending intense shock waves of electric pain up and down the length of the nerve bundles that service Keogh's damaged legs.

"Oh God," he says aloud, "get me out of here."

That's when the young, smooth-skinned native man holding the foot of the gurney to his right turns and shoots him a look.

"You must not talk," he speaks in a low, quiet, but somehow commanding voice. "You must save your energy."

"You speak English," Keogh comments through a cloud of cigar smoke. "But how can that be?"

"Yes." The man nods. "I was educated in Lima where I drove a taxi and kept an apartment for a time. I am a rare individual living inside this jungle. An educated man who deserted the concrete jungle to make his return to true civilization. Now please, rest. Soon we arrive at the Mouth of the Beast, and you will need all the strength you can muster."

"The Mouth of the Beast," Keogh repeats. "I'm not sure if I should be happy or frightened about going there."

Tossing what's left of his cigar over the side of the gurney into the leafy canopy far below, he lays his head back painfully into the cot. Soon, exhaustion sets in, and he is fast asleep once more.

The third and final time the Colonel lifts his head up, he is lying on the floor of a cave. The place is enormous. Cavernous. Dimly lit with at least two hundred burning torches mounted to the walls by means of heavy metal clamps. Something occupies the floor. Something big and bird-shaped. Excepting the three black, vertical legs and feet which extend down from its belly and beak, the object appears to be made of gold. The light from the torches makes the giant bird's golden skin glimmer brilliantly. Raising his hands to his eyes, Col. Keogh rubs the sleep out of them and takes a closer look. The object is not a bird, exactly, but something else.

"Well, I'll be a sad son of a bitch," he whispers. "It's a goddamned plane."

How the hell did a plane that big get all the way out here in the *jungle where there's no landing strips? How did it get up here in this cave? And if it's a plane, where are its propellers? He's heard talk about some experiments going on inside Nazi Germany with propellerless jet engines, but that's the stuff you find in the Buck Rogers Saturday afternoon movie serials.*

That's when something else comes to him.

He's not presently lying inside a naturally formed cave, so much as a natural cave that's been manually widened on both sides and extended deep into the heart of the mountain. Also, the ceiling has been raised while the floor has been smoothed out. The engineering he is witnessing is simply too incredible for words, be it ancient engineering or as modern as the day before yesterday.

Keogh is an experienced pilot and he knows an airplane hangar when he sees it.

"An airplane hangar all the way out here in the jungle. A hangar that houses a golden, bird-shaped plane with no propellers."

Four natives approach him, including the smooth-faced one who spoke English. They take their respective places and lift him up off the floor.

"Is that an airplane?" Keogh grunts through pain-gritted teeth as they begin to move in the direction of the big golden bird.

"The human beings here don't understand the word airplane," he explains, talking slow and softly over his left shoulder. "They only understand the concept of the bird. So that's what they call it."

"The bird."

"You would know this bird as a condor."

"But there are no condors in Peru. Only far up north and far down south."

"It is still a condor, Colonel. No matter how you look at it."

"It is a beautiful sculpture anyway. Magnificent even. How long has it been here up in this cave?"

"For many, many generations. So long, in fact, only the Gods would know for sure."

Keogh is stunned at the news. It would mean that the bird/plane would have been constructed in ancient times. But that's impossible.

6

"Who built her then?"

"So many questions from a man whose legs need emergency repair or else face the doctor's blade."

"I might be in pain, or even dying. But the still alive explorer in me is curious as all hell."

"No one knows who built her. Legend has it that she one day appeared above the jungle from out of the heavens, and landed in this cave."

"Wait. What do you mean landed? As in, that thing flew here?"

This time, the man turns all the way around so that he can look into Keogh's eyes.

"Yes, the bird flies. What other purpose would a bird's wings pose?"

Keogh can't believe what's coming from the man's mouth. It must be the stuff of legend and that's all. Modern flight wasn't tamed until thirty-seven years ago. If what this man is telling him is true, this "bird" must be thousands of years old. Yet he is insisting that it was flown here.

Having arrived at the bird, they come to a stop beneath the bird's belly. The English-speaking native issues a loud order in what Keogh recognizes as the ancient Incan language of Quechua, and just like that, everyone drops to their knees as if in reverence of something that's about to occur.

There comes a noise and loud bang that seems to make the cave rattle, and then a bright light emanates from the belly of the bird. The light is square-shaped as it beams from out of a big door that is being opened. The door is slowly opening from the top and lowering itself via hinges installed in its bottom, much like the bow door on a military cargo ship. When it is entirely opened, an amazed Keogh can see that the door also serves as an entry ramp.

"What in the world is happening?" he says.

"The bird not only flies," the English-speaking man whispers. "It contains tools and machines that can heal your legs quickly. Then, once you are rested, you will perform the sacred duty the Gods have brought you here to perform."

"And what duty is that, sir?"

"You will fly the Golden Condor back home for us."

"And where exactly is home?"

The man slowly raises his head, reverently looks up at the black cave roof, and smiles.

"The heavens," he says.

PART I

1

Bertelsmann Building, Times Square
New York City
May 2014

I don't just close the door to my agent's swank, fourteenth-floor office after entering into it for our scheduled 10 a.m. meeting. I lock it. I also don't bother with politely taking a chair in front of a glass desk that's so big and wide, a pilot flying over it might confuse it for a small lake if only a roof weren't covering this steel and concrete skyscraper.

Instead I go around the desk, set my callused hands on the narrow shoulders of Leslie Singer, my brown-eyed, long and dark-haired agent of nearly five years, and spin her around so that she faces me. Bending down, I plant a kiss on her thick, red lips.

Coming up for air, I look into her eyes and smile.

"Yes, you may kiss me," she says, her eyes wide and sparkling. "And do you know why you may kiss me, Chase? Because my gynecologist fiancé ... the very man who claims to love me and *only* me ... makes it a point to kiss and more than kiss every skirt he can get his hands on. Including his clients."

"Is this a bad time, agent lady?" I say, forcing a pretend frown. "Because I can go grab a cold shower and come back."

"You, client man, will remain right where you are. And that's an order."

That's when I squat at the knees, slip my arms under her legs, and lift her up onto the glass desk, knocking over a cup full of pencils and pens and sending two manuscripts onto the floor. Chase the wicked.

"I thought we arranged this meeting so we could discuss your future, Chase Baker," she says, her breathing growing heavy.

Looking down, I catch my reflection in the table top. I might have shaved and combed my hair once I landed this morning at JFK International Airport. But I like the scruffy look and my hair is so short these days a comb would be useless.

Leslie looks me up and down.

"Glad you dressed for the occasion," she says. "You dress just like The Man in the Yellow Hat from the *Curious George* books."

"Hey, I just got off a plane less than an hour ago," I say, patting the well-worn passport stored in my top left breast pocket. The pocket over my heart. "I haven't even seen my little girl yet."

"Who are you kidding?" she laughs. "You would have worn that getup anyway."

It's the truth and she knows it. What's also the truth is that I've just flown in from West Africa via Paris where I was on assignment for a glossy called *Living Ready* who hit me up for a survival in the bush story, pictures *and* words. While I survived the bush with little more than mosquito bites, the fifteen-hundred-buck payday barely covered my flights. But then, that's showbiz, as they say. But it does explain why I've arrived for my meeting not in a business suit but instead my red-clay-soiled cargo pants, ten-year-old lace-up Chippewa work boots, and black T-shirt under a *National Geographic* bush jacket, the sleeves rolled up all the way to my elbows.

On the other hand, the tall, thirty-something Leslie is looking stunning today in her black miniskirt and matching black silk blouse. With the skirt hiked up high on her thighs, I can see that her sheer black stockings are of the thigh-high variety. My favorite. They match the black lace push-up bra that's clearly visible beneath her blouse.

I kiss her again and pretend I don't notice the big giant engagement ring on the second finger of her left hand, her cheating gynecologist hubby already waiting for her arrival later this afternoon at his WASP-infected seaside Hamptons "escape."

"You called this meeting, Ms. Singer," I say. "Are we going to discuss my future or not?"

I proceed to unbutton her shirt, starting at the top and working my way down. But she pushes my hand away.

"Wait just a minute," she says. "My future husband may not be honorable, but I still haven't made up my mind if two wrong turns equal the right path." Then, as if she's suddenly made her decision, she reaches out for the phone, picks it up, and using her extended pinky finger punches 0. "Linda, no calls or interruptions until I give you the all clear. You got that? Good." She hangs up. Looking back into my eyes, she says, "You see that wood box on the end of the desk to your left?"

I look. "So what?"

"You'll find a couple of primo Cubans in there just for you. Thought you might enjoy a welcome back smoke." She slides down off the desk. "Go ahead. Light up while I freshen up."

Looks like two wrong turns does indeed equal the right path...

She comes around the desk and disappears into her private bathroom. I open the lid on the box, pull out a cigar, and cut away the end with the blade on the new pocketknife I picked up at the duty-free at JFK after mine was confiscated prior to boarding the plane in Paris. Digging around in a pocket on my bush jacket, I pull out a box of wood matches I snatched from a beachside watering hole in Cotonou, and fire the cigar up. Inhaling the good Cuban tobacco, I feel the soothing nicotine enter into my blood stream. If my nine-year-old daughter, Ava, were here, she wouldn't just pull the cigar out of my mouth, she'd probably toss a glass of water in my face.

"Are you begging for lung cancer, Daddy?" the long-brunette-haired future pop star would say.

I look out the window onto the towers that form the perimeter of Times Square.

"It's a beautiful spring day," I say, loud enough for Leslie to hear me through the door.

The door opens and she emerges looking even more ravaging than before.

"I'm overwhelmed by passion," she says, setting herself back onto the desk. "You may approach me now."

I go to her, as ordered.

She grabs hold of my bush jacket by its lapels, pulls it off, lets it drop to the floor. She pats the .45 that's shoulder holstered to my left ribcage.

"You bring a pistol to my office? How did you manage to get that through airport security?"

"What if we need to shoot our way out for some reason?" I say. "And I stored it in a locker at JFK prior to my departure for Africa."

"Good thinking," she giggles. "But I don't like guns. I mean, think about it. It's not like imminent danger surrounds us. I think you're living inside one of your novels."

I set my cigar on the edge of her desk, so that the burning end is facing outwards.

"Shut up and take me, Agent," I say.

She unbuckles my holster and the pistol falls. Then she pulls off my T-shirt, revealing a torso that's not too badly put together for a man of middle age—laceration, bullet, and burn scars be damned. I continue unbuttoning her shirt until it's dangling off her shoulders. That's when I allow gravity to work in my favor as it slides down her narrow back to the desk top. Reaching around I unbuckle her bra strap and allow the delicate garment to drop, revealing pert white breasts and perfect round nipples that stand at attention.

Bending slightly at the knees, I slip my hands into her lace black panties and slowly slide them down past her thighs, then down over her knees, taking my sweet time the whole way.

"Oh, before I forget, Chase," she says, her voice deep and breathy. "You have mail."

"Jeez, can it wait?"

The panties drop to her feet which are covered in black pumps. I drop down to my knees, pull off the underwear and both pumps all at once. I then begin kissing her stockinged legs, starting at her feet, progressing up her calves to her thighs. When my lips reach the point of her thighs where the stockings end and bare skin begins, she opens her legs for me. Not wide, but wide enough. Her breathing is harder now, and she's beginning to moan a little.

"Or maybe I should read my mail now?"

"Not on your life," she insists, placing her right hand behind my head, pushing me into her.

I go to town, as they say, with Leslie, no longer moaning, but crying out, loud enough to necessitate my reaching up with my hand, cupping her mouth. After a time her body begins to tremble and I know that my cue to stand has arrived. That's when she grabs hold of my belt buckle, unbuckling it. She unbuttons my pants, pushing them down. I enter into her and together, we rearrange her desk in ways she never might have imagined. The phone drops to the floor, and so do some manuscripts.

It's then, over Leslie's bare right shoulder, I see the letter. It's a plain white envelope that's addressed to me in blue ballpoint. I happen to catch the return address. It's from Lima, Peru. Now two things on my body are piquing with interest.

"Are you there yet?" Leslie screams into my hand.

"Yes," I say. "I'm almost there, Agent."

She thrusts her hips under me and more things drop off the desk. But I have no way of knowing what exactly as we both come to that special place together on Leslie's desk in the fourteenth-floor office of the Singer Literary Agency.

When we're done, I roll over onto my back on her big desk.

"That was wonderful," she says, not without a laugh.

"This is exactly the kind of shenanigans that can get a girl fired."

"Not me. I own the joint."

In my head I'm picturing three or four of Leslie's female assistants, or "girls" as she refers to them, positioned outside the office, their ears pressed up against the wood door.

"I forgot about that little detail. I'm a lucky man."

"Yes and no," she says.

"What's that mean?" I say, rolling onto my left shoulder, facing her.

"It means, Mr. Man in the Yellow Hat, that you need to start making some money. Or ..." She allows the notion to trail off.

"Or what?"

"Start thinking about going back to sandbagging."

"It's sandhogging," I correct. Then, "I thought *The Shroud Key* was killing it on the charts. I nearly got myself killed on my quest to find the mortal remains of Jesus Christ, and I thought the novel I wrote about it was a testament to my talents both as a writer and a daring adventurer." I smile for effect.

"You love yourself, don't you, Chase?"

"I aims to please, even if the person I'm pleasing is me."

"In all seriousness, *Shroud Key* is still selling well. Or *was* selling well anyway. But none of the books on your backlist are selling right now and you need a new novel, like right this very second. This isn't like the old days when you put out one manuscript every two years. Readers want three books per year."

"That might intrude upon my travel plans."

"That's the reality of the modern literary market, Chase. You seen your latest royalty statement?"

"That's your job to send it to me."

"I have. Your problem is, you don't read your mail. Snail or email. You'd rather be reading Arrival and Departure boards at airports."

"Explain."

"*Shroud Key* earned out its fifty-grand advance, but not much more. Meaning you need a new book."

"I hate advances."

"Think about going Indie after this one. You get to keep all your royalties. Minus my fifteen percent of course." She rolls over, smiles at me.

"And conjugal meetings."

"That too. Especially considering the fragile nature of my current relationship. But get that cute little ass of yours into a chair and start typing. Our living depends upon it."

"Might have to do some on-site research first."

"Where exactly this time?"

"It'll come to me."

She pokes me.

"Make sure it comes to you soon, Chase," she insists. "There now, agent/client pep talk officially over and done with."

"I have the best agent in the world," I say, kissing her gently on the mouth. "Too bad she's making the mistake of marrying a less than trustworthy gynie."

"Hey," she perks up, "with self-publishing all the rage these days, anyone who types the word 'spit' onto a series of blank pages sixty thousand times can get their book published. That said, literary agents aren't quite in demand like they used to be. A girl has to look out for herself."

"A summer estate in the Hamptons and a three-bedroom apartment on the Upper West Side. You've looked out for yourself pretty damned well, Agent."

"I, like you, Mr. Man in the Yellow Hat, am an explorer and a survivor."

"You're also an opportunist who's about to marry a total jerk."

"Look who's talking, grave robber."

"I don't rob graves. I unearth ancient antiquities for the purposes of study and on-site research for my novels."

"Dangerous work if you can get it."

"And this isn't? What if the gynie were to find out about us? He might come after me with a pair of stirrups." On instinct, I find myself sitting up. "You smell smoke?"

I look down at her. She's making a Samantha *Bewitched* gesture with the nostrils on her pretty little nose that tells me she also smells something she shouldn't be smelling at the present moment. Until she bounds up.

"Jesus, it's fire."

I slide off the desk, glance to my right, and immediately see that not only has the lit cigar fallen to the floor, but so has a stack of manuscript pages that are now ablaze. Some of the pages have drifted under one of the floor-to-ceiling drapes, setting it on fire.

"Don't look now, but it's about to flash."

The words aren't out of my mouth before the drape in the room's far left corner goes up, setting fire to the wooden bathroom door at the same time.

The alarm goes off, but the sprinklers don't come on. Leslie goes to the phone, shouts into it, "Linda, everyone out! We're on fire! We're right behind you!"

The fire quickly races across the ceiling and begins running down the wall that surrounds the office door. Our one and only way out of the office.

"Call 9-1-1," I order.

She pulls on her skirt, throws her shirt over her naked chest, buttoning the center button only. Picking up her phone, she dials 911.

"Phone's out!" she barks.

"Already?" I say, pulling on my pants and stepping into my

boots before putting on my bush jacket and pulling the .45 from its holster. "Here," I add, pulling out my cell phone from the jacket pocket and tossing it to her. "Use mine." That's when I notice the letter addressed to me from Peru. I snatch it up, stuff it into my jacket pocket before it too, ignites.

Taking the phone in hand, she dials 911. In the meantime, I go to the office door. But it's not only surrounded by fire, it too is now on fire. There's no way we're making it through there alive. I turn back to Leslie. She tosses me the phone.

"It's been called in," she informs as I snatch the phone from out of the heated air. "They're on their way." She smiles. "We're saved."

I look up at the ceiling. It's almost entirely covered in creeping fire. The wall behind me is also covered. Even the bathroom is engulfed in red/orange flames. In my head I'm calculating the chances of Leslie and me surviving the ten minutes it will take for the fire trucks to get here through the thick Manhattan traffic. The calculation I come up with is zero chance.

"Leslie, I want you to listen to me. This room is about to flash over. When that happens, it will literally cook us alive."

"What do we do?"

I hold up the .45.

"We shoot our way out. Right through that window."

Pointing the pistol barrel at the floor-to-ceiling glass, I pump the trigger. The room explodes in gunfire, causing Leslie to cover both ears with her hands.

"Told you we might need my gun," I shout, proudly observing the wide semicircle of bullet holes I've shot into the safety glass.

"Yeah, I feel much better now that you've shot the glass dead," Leslie says, with a roll of her eyes.

"Ye of such little faith," I say. Then, "Help me with something."

I go to her desk, positioning myself on the far right side of it. Leslie comes to me, stands beside me.

"When I give you the word, we're gonna push your desk through the window in the exact spot that I just carved out with my gun. You with me here?"

"You're the Man in the Yellow Hat. How could I not be with you?"

"Okay, grab hold." She does it. "Ready. Set. Go!"

Together we shove the heavy glass and metal desk across the smooth tile floor until it connects solidly with the bullet-weakened section of window. To my surprise and delight, the piece of window shatters on contact, sending millions of glass shards and the heavy desk sailing down into Times Square below.

"Christ, I hope we didn't just kill someone," Leslie moans.

"Chance we gotta take."

I go to the window, drop onto my knees, and look out. Fourteen stories down I can see the crowd of onlookers that has gathered in the streets to watch the inferno. I can also make out the now shattered desk and the many pieces of window glass. Luckily, I'm not seeing any dead or injured bodies. Unluckily, I'm not seeing any fire trucks. I don't need to sneak a look over my shoulder to see that the fire in the office is only growing in strength with the introduction of fresh oxygen.

"Leslie!" I shout above the fire's roar. "We don't have time to wait for the fire trucks. We gotta get out now."

"We can't just jump. We'll die."

She's right. We'll smack the concrete pavement and explode like water balloons.

I look down toward the street once more. That's when I see it. There's a series of balconies a couple of floors down. If we can somehow make it down to them, we'll be safe. But how the hell can we get there without rope?

I look to my left and see nothing but fire. I look to my right and see the same expanding fire. But at the same time, I see something else. The second set of floor-to-ceiling curtains. Miraculously, they have yet to catch fire.

Bounding up to my feet, I go to the curtains, yank them off their hooks in one swift pull. The top portion of the fabric is on fire. But I stamp it out. As I suspected, the fabric is far too thick for me to tear into with my bare hands. I need something to at least get it started.

Once again I pull out my pocket knife, dig out the blade, and proceed to make a cut in the top center of the long curtains.

"Help me tear these in two." I offer her one side of the curtain.

Leslie goes back down onto her knees, grabs hold of a chunk of curtain.

17

"Pull," I say and together we turn one long curtain into two long sections of curtain. Then I repeat the process two more times with each separate section of curtain, making four long strips in total. That done, I tie each section of curtain to the other using secure sailor's knots. In the end, I have about forty feet to work with, which should prove more than enough for descending two full stories.

"I need something to tie off to." I immediately begin looking around the fire-covered room.

"There isn't anything!" Leslie answers. "Chase, hurry. The heat is unbearable."

Wiping the sweat from my eyes, I look behind me at the broken window. It's then I see the piece of vertical aluminum window frame.

"That's it," I say, once more pulling out my .45, and shooting out a small concentrated area of glass that exists on the opposite side of the four-inch-wide piece of frame. The piece of glass disappears.

Shoving the gun in my jacket pocket, I slide the topmost portion of curtain through the small hole in the glass and tie it off around the frame. I yank on it to make sure it's secure and able to hold our collective body weight.

"Let's go!" I say, standing, the heat of the fire slapping me in the face.

"You mean, like out the window?" Leslie swallows.

"You got a better idea? We're burning up."

Just then, a section of ceiling drops down onto the office floor, sending up an explosion of flames. Leslie screams.

"Cover your eyes," I insist, pulling her tight against my chest, wrapping my arms around her. Then, pushing her away, "We stay here, we die. We climb down to that balcony down below, we at least have a chance at staying alive. Take your pick."

She looks at me. There's tears in her eyes. I can't be sure if she's crying or if the tears are the result of the fire irritating her tear ducts. Probably both.

"We live," she says.

I grab hold of the curtain and position myself, posterior first, outside the window, my booted feet planted flat and securely against the stone wall like a mountain climber preparing to descend a cliff side.

"Grab onto me, Leslie," I shout. "Do it now!"

She steps onto the ledge, looks down. Coming from down in Times Square, the collective roar of the crowd. We're making quite the spectacle. Another section of ceiling drops and explodes. The wall to Leslie's right collapses, sending a plume of fire sailing across the room. It blows Leslie into me, where she grabs hold of my chest.

"That's one way to get over your fear of heights," I shout.

"Just go!" she screams. "Before we both fall."

"Okay, baby, here we go!"

Together, we begin making our slow descent, one hand-under-hand and foot-under-foot length at a time.

"Hurry," Leslie shouts. "I don't think I can hang on for another second."

"You have to hang on, Agent. No choice."

An explosion comes from Leslie's office as it reaches flashpoint. Looking up, I see the ball of flame that spews out of the opening in the glass. It's then I know we've barely made it out alive. But then I can see that we're not that lucky. The top portion of curtain-rope is on fire. It won't take but a few seconds for the curtain to burn all the way through, sending us on a one-way ride to the pavement below.

It's taking all my strength, but I keep on descending past the set of windows on the thirteenth floor where a group of office workers are screaming through the glass, "You can make it! Go! Go! Go!"

Why the hell they haven't evacuated the building is beyond me.

Then we make it past the glass until we reach more exterior stone wall, and finally, down onto the balcony, where Leslie and I collapse onto one another, the now burnt-through curtain separating from the window frame above, floating down upon us, gently covering our bodies like a blanket I might lay out over my daughter before kissing her goodnight.

"I'd forgotten how much fun sex can be with you, Chase," she exhales after a time.

"I always make a point of pleasing my agent."

Just then, the sound of fire engines. Finally.

"'Bout time," Leslie says. "This is for saving my life, Chase Baker." She leans over me, plants a big wet kiss on my parched lips. The doors behind us slide open and a team of reporters begin flashing away. Behind them comes a team of firemen.

"Get back!" they shout. "These people are injured."

Leslie pulls herself off of me, holds up the hand that houses her engagement ring as if to say, "Don't shoot!"

"Hope the gynie isn't paying attention to the live news at noon," I say.

"The news is always on in his office," she says with a smirk. "Oh well, shouldn't come as a shock to him that he's not the only one who gets to play around."

"Looks like you're still not the marrying kind. We have that in common."

"Wish we didn't have it in common."

"Look at it this way. You would've been bored spending the rest of your life in the lap of luxury."

But Leslie doesn't laugh as the fireman helps her up off the balcony floor and leads her into the safety of the building. A hot New York literary agent who's just lost her business and her cheating beau in the time it takes to read *The End*.

2

Leslie and I are stuffed into the back of an EMT van which is headed to the nearest medical center. She sits directly across from me, looking more dejected than injured, elbows planted on her knees, her face propped up by her hands, her multi-carat engagement ring sparkling in the brilliant sunlight that, on occasion, shines through the windows, bathing the back bay in late spring's radiant warmth.

"So much for the Leslie Singer Literary Agency," she laments into her hands, her eyes now gazing down at her bare feet, neither her sexy black pumps nor her sheer, dark, thigh-high stockings having survived the fire. "I should have never allowed you to light up."

"Come on, that's no way to talk. You're the hottest agent in town. You're friends with the famous." I smile for effect. "Plus, you must be insured. You might end up making a profit in the end."

She doesn't look up. She doesn't move.

"Leslie," I say, as my smile dissolves. "You *are* insured, right? The Bertelsmann boys would never give you a lease without the proper insurance in place. I mean, I guess I never should have set a lit cigar down on the edge of your desk. At least, not immediately prior to engaging in wild sex atop it."

She's not moving, her eyes still locked on the top of her red, pedicured toes.

"You've got to keep up with your payments in order to be insured, Chase," she mumbles into her hands. "I've been walking a financial tightrope for ages now. Why do you think I've stayed engaged to a cheating fiancé for all these months?"

My heart aches for my agent.

"Do I get to ask why you didn't bother to pay your insurance payments?"

She looks up at me with her big, brown eyes.

"You have to be flush to do that."

"Leslie, you're one of the hottest agents in the business."

"Correction. *Was* one of the hottest agents in the business."

"I don't get it. What gives?"

"Take a look outside the window."

I shift in my seat so that I can look outside the side-panel window onto the many stores, eateries, bodegas, bars, and more that make up the pumping heart of mid-town Manhattan.

"Keep your eyes glued," she insists.

"Okay, what exactly am I looking at?"

"Keep looking. I'll tell you when we come to it."

The EMT van travels a full stop-and-go minute before my neck starts to ache. I turn back to her, pulling up the collar on my bush jacket, making sure it's buttoned, wishing my black T-shirt had made it through the fire unscathed.

"Give it to me straight, Agent."

"You happen to see a single bookstore while you were looking out the window?"

"Come to think of it. Not a one."

"Ten years ago you couldn't go half a block without seeing a bookstore, or a record store, or a video store. Sometimes you'd find all three times two on a single block. Now they are all as rare as a hailstorms. Maybe rarer."

Her words are like a light slap to my forehead. Why, as a writer, have I never noticed this rather sad phenomenon before now?

"Jeez, Leslie," I say. "You're right."

"Writers are dropping agents faster than landlords are cancelling the unpaid leases on independent bookstores."

"Why?"

"It's the digital age, Chase. Writers, songwriters, filmmakers, even video game designers are all DIYing it now. Cutting out the publishers altogether. And when the publishers get cut out of the loop, guess who quickly becomes an anachronism?"

"The deal-making literary agent."

"Exactly. Listen, I'm not saying I'm not making a living. But I've got a half dozen young ladies in my office who depend upon me. So when it comes to payday, I can either make out their paychecks or pay the insurance."

"You choose to pay them first. Why not cut down on staff?"

She purses her lips, glances down at her feet. "My heart goes out to them."

"Well, one thing's for sure, Sister Mary Leslie, you've got a heart of gold, but you're a shitty businesswoman. Do yourself a favor. Marry the rich gynie, even if he does dip his wick elsewhere."

"Thanks for the shitty advice. But it's a moot point anyway. I just got snagged kissing you on a balcony. The headline is probably all over Manhattan by now: Famous literary agent and famous writer nearly burn to death while getting laid."

We come to a sudden, jarring stop. The driver lays on his horn, then hits the sirens, then hits the horn again.

"Hell is going on?" I say, sliding out of my seat and opening the back bay door. I step out onto the shiny steel back bumper and make a quick survey of the situation. Up ahead on the narrow side street, a garbage truck is blocking all vehicular traffic.

"Thank God neither one of us is dying." I whisper, patting the Peru letter that's still stuffed in my chest pocket with my hand. Then, poking my head inside, "This is where I get off, Leslie."

I jump off the bumper, careful not to land on the front fender of the yellow cab that's pulled up on our tail.

"Chase," Leslie shouts. "What the hell are you doing? The hospital. We need to be checked out for injuries."

"I'm fine. Besides, I've got work to do. You said it yourself. It's either pull the typewriter back out or make a dismal return to sandhogging. Time to write another book." Once more slapping my chest pocket. "Who knows, this letter in my pocket might just hold the secret plot to my next bestselling novel. Or at the very least ..."

I'd finish my sentence if only the cabbie pulled up onto the

EMT van's tail doesn't lay on his horn.

"Jesus," I shout, as I turn, pull out my .45, aim it at the windshield of the yellow cab. The turban-wearing cabbie goes wide-eyed, holds up his hands in surrender. Then, turning back to Leslie, I stuff the gun back into my pocket.

"Or at the very least what, Chase?"

"Or at the very least, it might hold the secret to my future fortune and fame."

Shutting the bay door, I hop onto the cab's hood and make a flying leap onto the sidewalk.

Chase Baker, superhero.

3

Taking it double-time in the direction of downtown, I slip into a bodega where I purchase a black T-shirt that has the words NEW YORK CITY printed on the front in bright white letters. I pay the exorbitant twenty-five-dollar fee, then redress myself right on the spot, the Chinese vendor standing behind the counter shaking his head the entire time.

"What's the matter?" I say. "Never seen a grown man get dressed before?"

"No dress in public," he says in his heavily accented voice. "If you do that in my country, you get arrested."

"Welcome to New York," I say. "Anything goes."

I head back out of the store and continue toward downtown on foot. For a brief moment, I consider heading straight for Gramercy Park, where Ava lives with her mom and stepdad. But then just as quickly it dawns on me that she's still in school. I am, however, hungry. And when I spot a familiar corner diner I head inside, plant myself on a free stool at the counter, and order coffee, a plate of eggs over easy, and an order of lightly buttered wheat toast.

"What, no home fries?" says the tough, salt-and-pepper-haired waitress.

"No home fries."

"Why?"

"'Cause they suck."

She cracks a hint of a smile and leaves.

When she comes back with the coffee, she flips over my coffee mug and pours me a fresh cup. At the same time, I reach into my chest pocket, pull out the letter, set it down onto the counter beside the white coffee mug. Sipping my hot coffee, I stare at the address while trying to think about who I know down in Lima. I've been to Peru twice, both times as a sandhog. The first time, I was barely out of college and working for my dad's excavation company. The second time I was working for myself.

On the first dig we were going after a large dish supposedly made of solid gold and decorated with a thousand precious jewels including a blue diamond. Legend had it that the dish had been shipped over from Spain along with Pizarro and countless other treasures. The dish was said to be hidden somewhere in the depths of the Cuzco Cathedral.

We never did find the precious treasure even after a full week of government-supervised digging, but we did find a firefight in the form of some local Incan bandits who subscribed to both the Tupac Amaru Revolutionary Movement and the pro-Cuban Shining Path Movement. One late afternoon as we were packing it in, the terrorists invaded the site, guns ablazin' and MRTA bandannas wrapped around their faces. Turns out they were hoping to steal the priceless object for their own as payback for the Spanish conquistadors who unrightfully invaded Peruvian soil from the Incans while raping the women and pillaging the homes. As luck would have it, no one was killed, but the conflict was enough for the government to shut us down and send my dad and his crews packing back up to the US.

The second time I went to Peru to dig, the MRTA and the Shining Path were all but history thanks to new, stricter Peruvian anti-terrorism laws. Our mission at the time was to unearth the many mummified remains that were slowly being exposed due to the hastily retreating glaciers in the Andes Mountains.

I personally excavated a girl of about fifteen who had been brought up to the mountain by a local priest and her parents in order to offer her body and blood as a sacrifice to the Gods. When I removed the lid of the heavily constructed straw basket, she revealed herself to be a beautiful young woman with thick, dark, braided hair, rich olive skin, big eyes, round face, and luscious lips.

She was wearing traditional colorful robes and fur, lace-up boots. In one hand she held a bag of coca leaves and in the other, a bundle of flowers, the petals of which were still attached to the stems. After careful examination we could see that she'd been hit on the back of the head with a blunt object in order to render her unconscious. She was then left out in the elements to freeze to death. I recall shedding a tear as we loaded her tiny, but near perfect, six-hundred-year-old body onto a truck bound for the Cuzco museum.

Even with having worked those two sites in and around Cuzco and Lima, I still can't recall anyone I know well enough to be sending me a personal letter. That said, I steal another sip of coffee and decide once and for all to cut to the chase. Using the butter knife as a letter opener, I slide the blade inside the glued flap and slice it open. Setting the knife back down, I pull out the single piece of letterhead, the name Peter C. Keogh III gracing the top.

I look at the words written on the plain white, expensive stock.

"Meet me at JFK International for drinks and hors d'oeuvres. Gate 14B. Four o'clock. Don't worry about finding me. We'll find you."

It's signed *PCK III.*

My food arrives. The waitress sets it down, asks me if I need ketchup for the home fries.

"I didn't order home fries."

The waitress shoves a little pencil behind her ear, says, "Consider the home fries on the house. Now you want ketchup or not?"

"Sure, seeing as they're on the house and all."

"Everybody thinks they're Jim Carrey," she says, grabbing hold of a fire engine red squeezable ketchup bottle and slapping it down in front of me. "Bon appétit."

She walks away. Cutting a piece of egg and hot smooth yolk with my fork, I then set it onto the triangular edge of buttered wheat toast. Raising the toast to my mouth, I bite it off. The eggs are hot and delicious. I guess I should be nicer to the waitress.

Washing down my egg and toast with more coffee, I read the letter from PCK III again, and again, and one last time for good measure. The words don't change no matter how many times I read it.

Folding it back up, I stuff it back into the pocket of my bush jacket and think. Why would this PCK III character want me to meet him at the airport? Why not meet at a restaurant or bar like civilized people? Shit, why not call or email? What if I simply ignore him and don't do anything?

Certainly, judging from the expensive stationery and the name snazzily printed on it, Mr. Keogh is civilized enough. He also assumes that me being me, I'll be curious enough not to blow him or his invitation off. But then, I get the feeling he's not your everyday kind of average Joe either. In fact, if I listen to my gut, it seems to keep on repeating the same words over and over again: Mr. PCK III is richer than Jesus. And maybe even as important. In certain circles, that is.

"Well, one thing's for sure, Mr. Keogh," I say, out loud, "you've piqued my interest much more than the home fries have."

"Excuse me?" says the waitress.

"Oh," I say, holding out my coffee cup, "you mind warming this up for me, pretty lady?"

She comes back over with the pot of coffee.

"Who you callin' pretty?" she says, pouring more coffee into my cup.

"Term of endearment," I say.

"Tell that to my girlfriend." Then, "How them home fries treatin' ya?"

"They're free," I say. "No complaints."

"You're right," she says before walking away. "Home fries suck."

4

Coming out of the diner, I make a check on the time.

It's already half past one in the afternoon. I have just enough time to get home, get cleaned up, and think about hiring a driver to take me out to JFK for four o'clock. So much for seeing my little princess as soon as school lets out. I hope ol' PCK III won't mind reimbursing me for the cost. Making my way to the street corner, I hail a taxi to take me the rest of the way downtown.

Opening the back door, I go to step in when somebody shoves up against me.

"Excuse me, my friend," he says. "But are we not heading the same direction? Perhaps we should cut our expenses in two and share this cab."

I'm a resident of two cities. Florence, Italy, and New York City. In Florence, the taxi cabs are white Mercedes Benz wagons. Oftentimes a driver might be a well dressed gentleman whose extended family has, for generations, devoted themselves to the noble pursuit of driving. Sometimes the drivers are even women, beautifully and expensively attired. When hailing one of these drivers, under no circumstances would another customer be rude enough to jump in front of you suggesting you share the ride.

But in New York City, where most of the cab drivers don't speak English, it's not all that uncommon for a man or woman to jump in front of you, hop in, shut the door, and steal the cab ride altogether. I'll say it again: In NYC, anything goes. Most anything anyway. The fact that this little, neatly dressed, bald-headed man suggested we share the ride proves at least a semblance of good manners. I decide to reward him with a monotone, "Okay."

We both get in.

"Corner of Prince and Houston," I say to the driver.

"That's fine with me," confirms the little man.

Like I said, he's bald, but neatly kept. He's wearing a lightweight baby blue suit that looks like it came from Brooks Brothers, and loafers with no socks. The knot on his red and white necktie is perfect, his pink oxford impeccably pressed. I peg him for late thirties, but he's so small and boyish looking, he could easily be ten years older or younger.

"Wish I could have a cigarette," he says in a voice that's neither masculine nor feminine, but somewhere in between. The accent is not American. At least, not US, but Latin American. Which country it originates from I can't be sure, however.

"Was a time not too long ago," I say, "a blue cloud of cigarette smoke hung over Manhattan."

"Filthy disgusting habit anyway." The Peter Lorre look-alike smiles, looking up at me with big, dark, round bulbs for eyes. "My mother died from the big, grotesque tumors that formed on her lungs from a three pack a day habit. She was a sweet woman, my mother. Died far too young."

"I'm sorry," I say, focusing my attention out the window onto the fenced-in Gramercy Park where my princess resides, feeling the pangs of missing her like stones in my stomach. "Maybe you should quit too, before the same fate awaits your lungs."

I'm not entirely sure why I'm engaging in a conversation about life or death with this man, but somehow, it seems like it would take more effort to ignore it.

He goes on, "Oh, but I have a plan should that eventuality raise its ugly head."

I turn back to him.

"A plan." It's a question.

"Did you know that there are doctors in South America and other parts of the world who can cure tumors with their hands?"

"No, I didn't."

"Oh, but it's true. Just last month a team of three medical

doctors in Beijing were able to cure a woman's breast cancer by placing their hands on her body for a period of an hour. The entire procedure was recorded with an MRI. Do you have any idea how long it took her multiple tumors to disappear?"

"No idea, pal."

"Less than three minutes."

I laugh. "Listen, little friend, don't you think if something that miraculous were to truly have occurred that it would gain top billing in the world news?"

He nods, emphatically.

"Precisely," he explains. "But here in the West, we have trouble believing that one man's positive healing energy can be transferred into another sicker individual just through something as simple as touching. Yet the ancients have known about this secret for millennia. The mainstream media refuses to report on these miracles simply because they fear for their credibility."

"And how did the ancients come to know about this healing energy you speak of?"

"It is possible the ancient astronauts taught us."

"Astronauts from ancient times." I snicker. Okay, maybe I'm laughing at the concept of ancient astronauts, but I'm not about to discount the possibility of their existence either. After all, who in the past has gone in search of God and aliens and uncovered enough evidence to back the existence of both? Maybe even evidence to prove that they are one and the same? That who is me.

"Yes, ancient astronauts, hard to believe," he goes on. "But as time goes on, scientists are discovering more and more about ancient civilizations. The Egyptians, the Romans, the Incans, the Chinese, the Asian Indians, and the American Indians were far more advanced than for which written history gives them credit. There's proof of them harnessing electricity, of conquering the skies with man-made flying objects, and even harnessing the power of healing."

"Fascinating," I say, still playing dumb as the taxi pulls up to the corner of Prince and Houston.

The dark-skinned driver turns around.

"Twelve dollar," he says in a heavy accent that could be Afghan as easily as it could be Pakistani.

"You wanna split it, little buddy?" I say, reaching into my

pocket for some cash.

But the bald man is too quick. He's already pulled a ten and a five from his billfold, and is handing it to the driver through the Plexiglas opening over the seatback.

"Please keep the change," he insists to the driver in his soft, strange voice. Then, turning back to me, he holds out his right hand. "I am Carlos," he says, while reaching into his suit jacket with his free hand, pulling out a business card and handing it to me.

I take the small, almost birdlike hand in mine, give it quick squeeze and a shake, then pocket the card without looking at it.

"I'm Chase," I say. "Chase Baker."

"But of course you are. Pleased to meet you, Chase. If you would ever like to talk more about the ancients and their mysteries, do not hesitate to give me a call. And thank you again for allowing me to share your cab."

I watch him open his door, get out, and disappear around the corner. Opening my door, I step on out, shutting the door behind me. As I start walking toward my small apartment above the Italian restaurant on Prince Street, I can't help but wonder if it's entirely coincidental that Carlos and I shared the cab ride together, or if the strange man's sudden appearance in my life was planned that way all along.

5

Walking.

I've traveled enough in my life to know that you don't always get around this big blue planet by means of a map or compass or even GPS. You get around by listening to your gut. And right now, as I walk the busy downtown Manhattan street, I'm once again listening to my gut speaking to me loud and crystal clear. It's telling me, *"Don't look now, Chase, old boy, but you are being followed."*

It's not just the voice that alerts me. It's also the dryness in my mouth, the tightness in my stomach, and the fine hairs on the back of my neck that stand up at attention.

I don't dare gaze over my shoulder.

Not yet.

I keep walking like I'm oblivious. Just another chump making my way back to my apartment after a long trip, hoping the two bags (my North Face Venture 90 and my twenty-year-old Tough Traveler shoulder bag) I had sent on to my apartment from the airport will have arrived before I do. But then, quite suddenly, I stop and about-face.

That's when I spot him.

The strange little man in the blue suit ducking into a dark alley.

6

I don't hesitate to go after him.

Breaking out in a sprint, I head for the alley opening, dodging the innocent bystanders who block my path by running around them or simply pushing them out of the way. When I come to the alley, I stop and pull out my .45, thumbing off the safety. I gaze into the empty, shaded alley. Two tall brick walls flank me. Moisture and damp drip from numerous metal downspouts. Rusted, over-filled dumpsters occupy the long runway. I hear a noise and a commotion coming in the direction of the first dumpster. Raising the gun, I plant a bead on it. But that's when I spot a rat the size of a house cat pop its head out, its nose whiskers twitching as it pushes aside an empty box and some newspapers, then jumping down into the alley, scattering off for the protection of a hole in the wall.

I step inside the alley, hearing my footsteps echoing against the brick walls. Then, up ahead, a man scoots across the width of the alley. He opens a door and enters into a building. It's him. The bald man in the blue suit.

I give chase.

I find the door, grab hold of the opener, and twist. But it's locked.

"Son of a bitch," I whisper to myself. Looking over one shoulder, then the other, I plant the barrel of the .45 against the opener and press the trigger. The lock shatters into so many metal fragments. Pulling the metal door open, I'm greeted with a set of concrete and metal stairs. I bound up them two at a time, until I come to the first landing. I see him looking down at me through the opening in the center of the wraparound staircase.

"Wait," I shout. "Stop!"

But he keeps running up the stairs. I follow, gaining on him with my every lunge. Apparently he smokes too much, because it doesn't take me long to shorten the distance between us by only a single staircase. He knows I'm gaining on him, because instead of climbing more stairs, he scoots off to the right, bolts through another door.

I shoot up to the door and throw it open before he has a chance to lock it. But it doesn't matter. Because now I find myself inside a crowded department store. Not just any department store, but one that specializes in Asian products. This must be the self-defense department, because the walls are filled with perfect replicas of ancient weapons. From where I am standing, I spot qiang spears, jian and dao swords, and flying knives.

Stepping into the open store, I pocket my .45 before someone spots me with it. I scan the store with my eyes, but I don't see the little man. Is it possible he got away? I walk up one aisle and down another, and still he is nowhere to be found. For a time, I hold my ground and simply observe. But after a period of five minutes or so, I decide to head back the way I came and abandon the search, chalking the whole experience up as just another strange occurrence.

I head back across the floor and enter into the back, off-limits hallway, until I come to the emergency exit. Placing my hand on the opener, I'm about to open the door, when a flying knife impales itself into the thick wood.

7

"Don't turn around, Mr. Baker," comes the odd, nasally voice I've come to recognize in a very short time. "Don't even breathe or I will destroy your liver."

I feel the sharp tip of a second flying knife pressed against my abdomen.

To the right of the exit door I spot another door. It says For Employees Only. I can't be sure, but if I had to guess, it's a bathroom. The bald man is smaller than me, thinner. I'm wondering if he's quicker too.

Only one way to find out.

Spinning fast, I grab hold of his wrist. I squeeze the wrist hard and the knife falls from his hand to the concrete floor. Then, reaching into my pocket, I grab the gun, thumb back the hammer, press the barrel to his now sweat-soaked forehead.

"Let's take a powder, Baldy," I say, pulling him into the bathroom.

I lock the deadbolt before dragging the bald man to the toilet.

"Knees," I bark.

"Please, Mr. Baker," he says. "I was only doing my job."

"Knees," I say again. Sharper this time, while thrusting my right knee into the back of his knee, collapsing him entirely.

Since he's got no hair for me to grab hold of, I grab the collars on his suit jacket and oxford button-down and shove his head into the toilet. I hold him there for maybe five or six seconds until he begins to cough and choke. Then I pull him back out.

"Who do you work for? And why are you following me? Sharing cab rides with me?"

He takes a minute to catch his breath, his face soaking and dripping in toilet water.

"Chase, you hate me, don't you?" His words are choking out of him along with the rancid water.

"I don't even know you, pal, which is kind of the point." Pushing him back toward the bowl. "Now tell me what I want to know or drown."

I push, but as his head descends beyond the bowl's rim, he cries, "Wait. Please, wait."

I pull him back out.

"You ready to talk?"

"I was sent to take care of you."

"I can see that. So who sent you?"

He hesitates.

"Tell me," I insist, pushing his head back toward the bowl.

"Keogh."

I have to think for a brief moment, but then it comes to me. The letter inside my bush jacket pocket. Or, the invitation for drinks at JFK, I should say. Why would Peter Clark Keogh the Third graciously invite me for drinks only to sic one of his goons on me? I have an idea or two.

"Let me guess, Baldy," I say, "your boss, PCK the Third, was afraid I might not show."

"Something like that," he whispers.

"Threatening me with flying knives your idea of persuasion?"

"I was afraid you might disappear now that you knew I was following you. My mistake, Mr. Chase. Please forgive me."

I let him go.

"Get up, Baldy," I say, returning the hammer to the safety position on the .45, but keeping it gripped in my hand. "Clean up."

He slowly stands, goes to the sink. First he washes his face and head with soap and water, then he dries himself with paper towels. He finishes by straightening his tie and his suit jacket so that it's as perfect as possible.

"You're a funny little man, Baldy," I say. "I really should kick the living snot out of you and then tell PCK the Third to go fuck himself. But since my gut tells me he's got more pretty green than Trump and he wants my attention so badly he's willing to have me followed, I can't help but be more than a little curious."

He turns, smiles half-heartedly with his thin bee-lips.

"I shall arrange our transportation," he says. "Where shall I pick you up?"

"No dice, Baldy," I say. "Where's your boss now?"

"Inbound," he says, "from Berlin."

"Man who likes to get around. I like PCK the Third already. Tell you what. We're not going to wait until four o'clock. You and I are going to see him now."

"But it is his habit to shower and nap after a long flight. He is not a well man these days."

"He can shower after I'm gone," I say, unlocking the deadbolt. Then, waving the pistol barrel at him, "Let's get a move on, Baldy."

He brushes past me, opens the door.

"Mr. Chase," he says, "would it be terribly inconvenient for you to refer to me by my Christian name?"

I slip the .45 into my bush jacket pocket.

"I'm kind of getting used to Baldy, Carlos."

"As you wish," he says.

Together, we head for the back staircase while I silently make the decision to can the Baldy crap.

8

Carlos pulls his cell phone from his pocket, makes a call. Within three minutes, a big black sedan with tinted windows pulls up to the corner of Prince and Houston.

"Excellent service," I say.

Carlos opens the back door for me.

"After you," he insists, smiling that bee-lipped smile again.

"You first," I say, reaching into my pocket, pressing the barrel of the .45 outward so that it tents the fabric. "I've had enough surprises for one day."

"Of course," he says, slipping inside.

I follow.

The driver sitting behind the wheel is big and bulky. He's wearing a black suit and his thick dark hair is slicked back with product. His eyes are covered with aviator sunglasses.

"Mr. Keogh has just landed, Carlos," the driver says into the rearview. "Will you be notifying him of our early arrival?"

"I've already forwarded a text."

With that, the driver pulls away from the curb and heads for the Williamsburg Bridge which will take us to the expressway that eventually hooks up with JFK International on Long Island. On the way, I send Leslie a simple text: "How are you?"

"I'll live. But my business is dead."

"I'm sorry," I type in with my thumbs, picturing the long-haired agent sitting on her couch in her robe, having just showered, a full glass of blood-colored Merlot set out before her. "Plans?"

"Chill. Try and figure out the best way to pawn my diamond."

"Uh-oh. He saw the news."

"He asked me for the truth. I asked him for the same."

"Sorry times two."

"Where are you?"

"On way to JFK."

"Leaving town so soon?"

"Meeting the mysterious Peru letter man for drinks."

"He's flying in to meet you? Must be important."

"Whatever it is, I hope there's lots of money involved."

"I'll say a novena."

"Do me a favor."

"Anything for you Chase (chills going up and down my spine)."

"LOL. Stay close to the phone. I don't know who these people are. I might need you."

"I'm your babe, Chase Baker."

"I almost feel sorry for the gynie."

I pocket the cell phone.

We arrive some sixty stop-and-go minutes later. The driver pulls up to Terminal 4, Delta's international terminal, and we get out.

"I'll text you when we're done," Carlos informs the driver before closing the door. Then, to me, "This way, Mr. Chase."

We proceed through a pair of sliding glass doors and enter into a crowded, high-ceilinged airplane hangar of a building.

Carlos holds out his hand.

"Your sidearm, please," he says, with a straight face.

"Hey, Carlos, I'm not that kind of guy—"

"I understand you carry the proper credentials on your person. But it will be much easier for us to get where we're going if you're not carrying a gun."

Reluctantly, I reach into my pocket, hand it to him, grip first.

"Thank you," he says, taking the gun in hand, slipping it into his jacket pocket. "Wait here."

Before I have a chance to argue, he slips away into the crowd.

A few minutes later he returns. In his hand is a key to a locker. He hands it to me.

"12C," he says. "Should anything happen to us, the lockers are located along the far west wall of the terminal. But then you surely know that already."

"What can possibly happen to us?"

"Anything, I'm afraid."

"Good to know," I say, as I follow him toward an overhead sign that reads, "All Gates."

9

Having made our way flawlessly through safety inspection, we then move on to one of the Delta gates. Gate 35 to be precise. There to greet us is an attractive flight attendant. Tall, shapely, with long straight blond hair, the blue-miniskirted attendant unlocks the metal door and leads the way along the enclosed gangway. When we come to the end of the ramp, we don't enter into an airplane, but instead are instructed to exit through a narrow door, then climb down the metal stepladder onto the tarmac.

As we descend the ladder I can't believe the vision that appears before my eyes. It's a relic of a World War II–era bomber. A B-52 Stratofortress to be precise, preserved in perfect condition. Its metal siding glistens in the afternoon sun as two of its four massive propellers come to a stop. While ground crew place chalks under the old plane's big black rubber tires, Carlos and I begin making our way toward it.

"You've got to be kidding me, Carlos," I say. "How did PCK the Third get his hands on one of these babies?"

"It's his office, actually," the bald man informs, as we enter the area directly beneath the fuselage. "Mr. Keogh is a bit of a World War II aviation buff, as you can plainly see. He also owns a Spitfire and an Me109. Like his father before him, Mr. Keogh was an aviator before becoming an entrepreneur. He flew fighters in Vietnam."

"No shit," I whisper under my breath. "I'm beginning to like Keogh more and more."

Suddenly, a big square panel opens up on the belly of the fuselage. A young black man sticks his head out. He's clean shaven and wearing only a crimson T-shirt that fits so tightly to his massive biceps and chest that it might as well be a second skin.

"Carlos," he barks. "Turn that bald bulb of yours off. It's hurting my eyes, bro."

"Very funny, Rodney," Carlos responds. "This is Mr. Baker. He's arrived for the meeting."

The upside down Rodney glances at his wristwatch.

"Little early isn't it, Baker?" he comments.

"Blame the bald guy," I say, raising up my left arm, cocking my thumb at Carlos.

"Figures," Rodney says. "Let me get the ladder."

Rodney disappears back up into the belly of the beast. But a few seconds later, he lowers a metal ladder.

"Let's go, gentlemen," he says. "Mr. Keogh needs his rest so let's get this show on the road."

As I climb the ladder, I can't help but think, *PCK the Third likes to sleep a lot.* But as we climb into the old bomber and enter into the main cabin, I can see why. At the aft end of a cabin that's been renovated to resemble a rich man's smoking room complete with cherry wood paneling and a black and white tile floor, a tall, thin man sits in a leather easy chair. There's a black, plastic and metal mechanical device that resembles a vital functions monitor planted beside him. A series of clear plastic tubes extend from it. The tubes look as though they are inserted into the veins on his inverted left arm via numerous needles.

The man is pale and sickly, but somehow sharp looking in his neatly pressed khaki trousers, blue blazer, and brown-, yellow-, blue-, and red-striped rep tie. The tie is also ornamented with the silhouette of a red, naked, haloed woman who stands before a bright yellow star while joyfully waving her left hand.

"Mr. Baker," PCK the Third says with a deep voice. A voice that is surprisingly strong considering his physical condition. "Glad you could make it."

"The Flying Tigers," I say, nodding at his neck tie.

"I see you're schooled in your World War Two aviation

history," he says with a smile while holding out his right hand. "That's certainly a plus in my book."

Leaning down, I take hold of his right hand with my own. His grip is cold and tight for a man who isn't well. We shake once and release our hold on one another.

"You'll have to excuse the cryptic nature of my operation," he says. "It's, how shall we say, cloak and daggerness."

"That's one way of putting it."

"I trust you've become acquainted with my associate, Carlos."

"Very well acquainted indeed," I smile, shooting the little bald man a look.

"Carlos is a tad tenacious in his work," Keogh explains, his stunningly blue eyes also locked on Carlos. "He likes to pretend he's playing the role in a detective novel. Perhaps one written by Chase Baker himself."

"You a fan, Mr. Keogh?"

He nods.

"Most certainly," he says. "Since the onset of my cancer almost two years ago, I spend a lot of time sitting at this infernal machine. I try and spend that time wisely by catching up on my reading."

"I'm honored."

"I also understand you are in the possession of many talents, Mr. Baker. A true Renaissance man if ever there was one."

"Thank you for saying so. Which talent are you interested in today, Mr. Keogh?"

"I would like you to find something for me."

Behind my left shoulder stands Rodney, his arms crossed over his massive iron-pumped chest. Standing behind my right shoulder is Carlos, who exists as Rodney's polar opposite on planet earth. Apparently the only thing they have in common is their employer.

"I'm listening, Mr. Keogh," I say, glancing at the clear fluid that runs through the tubes into and out of his veins.

"Have you ever been to Machu Picchu, Mr. Baker?"

"Please call me Chase."

"Indeed, and please call me Pete."

"Sure, Pete." Then, "Machu Picchu? Never. Although I have worked in Peru a couple of times as a sandhog."

"Yes, I'm aware of that," he says. "You helped uncover some of the famous mummies of the Andes which are now stored in the

Cuzco Museum."

I nod.

"What I'll be looking for you to uncover might be a tad more difficult than that expedition."

"I'm still listening."

He raises up his free hand.

"Rodney, if you don't mind."

"Right away, Chief," Rodney says, hitting a switch on the wall which causes a flat-screen HDTV to lower itself from the cabin ceiling. Flashing onto the screen is a full-color 3D representation of Machu Picchu and the surrounding Urubamba River Valley which is a part of the Amazon basin, or what's sometimes referred to as Amazonia.

"As you can see, the excavated portion which was discovered by the explorer Professor Hiram Bingham in 1911 is the area typically visited by thousands of visitors each day, seven days a week, three hundred sixty-three days a year." Pointing to the green area beside the mountain peak. "But it's this area I'm interested in. The other seventy percent or so of the mountain and its neighboring Huayna Picchu to the right. This part of the mountain and its associated valley are still unexplored."

"Certainly indigenous Incans live there," I say.

"To be sure, and there are said to be many trails that cut through the thick vegetation. But no one dares access them for fear of these same tribal peoples."

I laugh. "Is that your nice way of saying people are still afraid of head hunters in the Amazon jungle?"

He cocks his head.

"Perhaps," he says. "But if I were a betting man, I wouldn't wager against their existence. Indeed, my own father may have met his own fate at the hands of these head hunters."

"Your father," I say like a question.

"Yes," he says. "My father."

Now on the television monitor is the figure of a handsome, if not dashing man dressed in long leather coat, leather flier's cap, tall boots, and khaki pants. He's smiling for the camera with the same blue eyes and mouth that his son now possesses, while he stands to the right of the propeller that belongs to his 1930s-era biplane.

"That's a de Havilland," I say. "Probably 1935, Tiger Moth model."

"Right you are again, Chase," Keogh says. "Back in 1939, my father was hired by Standard Oil to explore this uncharted territory for existing trails that might provide an accessible ground route into the Amazon basin. He was convinced that he could find it by engaging in low-level flights that began at the uncharted side of Machu Picchu and continued all the way into the basin. He would record these paths on film and then bring the proof with him back to Texas."

"I'm sensing a big 'But' coming up."

"But, he encountered a problem. He flew too low and crashed into the trees. I never saw him again. In fact, no westerner would ever see him again."

"Did he perish in the crash?"

He shakes his head.

"Not at all. In fact, he survived and lived long enough to produce this." He shoots Rodney a look. In turn, the beefy employee makes his way toward the plane's cockpit, but stops short of it at a bulkhead wall. Removing a small mirror from the wall, he reveals a safe. Typing in a code, the safe door opens. He reaches in and grabs hold of something, which he carries back out to us. What he's carrying is entirely familiar to me and most of the world.

It's a Coca-Cola bottle.

Rodney hands me the 1930s-era vintage Coke bottle. Back then the bottle was not only made of real glass but the words Coca-Cola were embossed into the thick glass itself. There's something stuffed inside the bottle. A large piece of paper that's been rolled up to fit through the bottle neck and that's browned over time.

I lock eyes with Peter Keogh III.

"What's this?" I laugh. "An honest to goodness message in a bottle?"

"I'll do you one better, Chase."

"How's that?"

"What you are holding in your hand is a genuine treasure map."

"Treasure map," I say, feeling my pulse speed up. "No shit."

"No shit, indeed," Keogh says with a laugh. "You, Mr. Baker, have entered into the no shit zone."

10

"Be careful of that," Keogh goes on. "It's very old."

Rodney hands me a pair of white gloves which I slip on before sliding the paper out of the bottle. Gently I unroll it and discover a hand-drawn map.

"I'm allowing you the pleasure of viewing and touching the real thing," Keogh explains. "I'm well aware of your love of antiquities, Chase. But my team has assembled a comprehensive computer-generated map for your smartphone and/or iPad for your real-time use in the field."

"iPads, real-time, smartphones … Sounds rather unromantic, doesn't it?" I point out while peering up from the old map.

"Perhaps one hundred years from now, it will be a different story."

"That is, if the earth *lasts* another one hundred years."

I take a moment to examine Keogh the Second's crude map. It's not very detailed. Fact is, it's altogether sparse in detail. Depicted on the upper left-hand side of the paper is Machu Picchu, its very vertical, exposed granite, needle-like summit clearly recognizable. Taking up the middle portion of the map is a narrow trail that snakes itself through what is clearly Keogh II's translation of thick growth, since the open space surrounding the trail has been shaded to near black with pencil. Taking up the entire right edge of the paper is a river. The words "Amazon River" have been penciled vertically into the center of the river in Keogh's rather fanciful handwriting.

But what interests me is what's depicted about three-quarters of the way across the map, looking from left to right. It's another mountain, the tall, needle-shaped summit of which is not altogether different from Machu Picchu's. What's mind-blowing is that there's a man-made staircase that corkscrews itself all around the mountain and that leads to a large opening, which Keogh describes simply as "Cave."

At the very bottom of the map, in the lower right-hand corner, is an area that's been boxed off. A heading appears at the top of the box. It says CAVE in large capital letters. There's no doubt in my mind that this is Keogh's way of offering a sort of crude, 3D blowup of the cave's interior. While the artistry is a far cry from 3D, there's no disputing the identity of the object that takes up the very center of the cave.

It's a huge bird.

"If that's a real condor nesting inside that cave," I say, "it would have to be as big as a dinosaur."

Keogh smiles as though in full agreement.

"Rodney, if you please," he says.

"If you wouldn't mind placing the map back inside the bottle, Mr. Baker," the big man asks, while holding out his bear-like hands.

I roll the map up, gently place it back through the bottle neck, and hand it on to Rodney. I also peel off the gloves and hand those to him too. As he makes his way back across the cabin to place the bottle back inside its safe, another image appears on the HDTV. It's a precise copy of Keogh's father's map. But unlike the original, this map has been digitally enhanced, making it go from crude drawing to detailed chart complete with GPS coordinates, 3D geographical imaging, and color-coded enhancement in order to separate those areas with heaviest vegetation from the more sparsely covered areas, including existing walkways and paths.

"As you can see from this new map," Keogh III explains, "the very trails my father was hired to uncover did indeed exist. Problem is, he had to crash in order to find them."

"Did anyone ever try to find your father after he went missing?"

"After the map was discovered washed up on the shores of the

Urubamba River, a rescue party was sent out after him, but not a single man returned. A few months later, a native emerged from the forest. He was wearing a ceremonial necklace that was said to contain the six shrunken heads of all the expedition members. A second expedition was not attempted."

"I can see why," I say, trying to conjure up an image of a half dozen shrunken heads hanging from a man's neck by a leather necklace. "But your father's head was never discovered, shrunken or otherwise?"

"Strange, isn't it?" he says. "But perhaps not so strange. I can only assume he was injured in the crash, survived for a time long enough to draw this map, and then perished. More than likely, some of his flesh was consumed by the cannibals as part of a ritual that would have included the burning of his body as an offering to a very special God."

"What God?"

"The God of the sky. The same God who makes lightning. His name is Apocatequil."

I nod. "Which, I'm guessing, is where the big bird comes in. The condor."

"Not just any condor, Chase. That's not a real bird my father discovered."

"If it's not a real bird, then what the hell is it?"

"Let's put it this way. When was the last time you saw a bird with an elevation rudder?"

I glance at the drawing of the bird as depicted on Keogh II's map once more. For certain the "bird" contains a rudder, much like a modern airplane.

"The condor is not a real bird then?" A question for which I'm already discerning the answer. Or Keogh III's version of an answer anyway.

"It's an aircraft, Chase. A one-thousand-year-old flying machine."

11

For a silent moment, I try to allow the concept of a one-thousand-plus-year-old flying machine to sink in. Keogh must see the doubt in my eyes, because he raises his right hand up as if pointing to the sky.

"Is the reality of an ancient flying machine really so hard to believe?" he begins to explain. "There's a tremendous amount of knowledge that has been lost through the ages and the harnessing of flight could very well be one of them. Ancients like da Vinci recognized that flight was indeed possible when he engineered his early flying machines back in the fourteen hundreds. The ancient Asian Indians also believe that flight was not only possible, but that their Gods were able to travel to and from earth via spaceships called Vimanas that spewed forth fire and smoke. Great battles between these spaceships are described in precise detail in ancient Indian Sanskrit texts dating back six thousand years."

"But what about the ancient Incans? How is it possible that a primitive jungle tribe who didn't even harness the concept of the wheel could engineer an airplane?"

"They didn't. Someone else did it for them."

"Who then?"

"Ancient astronauts."

The interior of the B-52 falls so silent that we can easily make out the thrusting of the jet engines on the airport's outbound planes.

Keogh III goes on, "Before you discount the idea, there are those who believe we are a species with amnesia. That there is a missing link in humankind's continuum—a place where the story of our history comes up blank. Many believe that the ancients were far more technologically advanced than for which we give them credit. That's where ancient aliens come into play. These ancients Gods, if you like, visited the earth many millennia ago and gifted our rather ignorant and primitive species with incredible gifts of knowledge. Not the least of which was how to construct an airplane. Problem is, no evidence of these aircraft has ever existed until my father stumbled upon it in 1939. Only peripheral evidence has been discovered, such as the Nazca lines which can only be discerned from high up at a great altitude."

On the TV monitor now, a video of the Nazca lines is playing. The lines are being filmed from the cockpit of a modern airplane but even then, it's not difficult to gain a sense of how massive the line drawings are. There's a spider, a monkey, a snake, and more.

"On the ground, the lines appear to be nothing more than one rock placed beside another. But from the air they appear in their true form. I believe, as do many others, that the lines were utilized as landing beacons for the incoming craft of the ancient astronauts. Indeed, located directly beside the Nazca lines are long runways that have been smoothed out of the rocky, gravelly soil. Some of the runways gradually increase in height in proportion to length, as to assist in the deceleration of landing high-speed aircraft."

"So what you're saying, Pete, is that the evidence has always been there. Just not direct evidence of an aircraft."

"Exactly," he says, as the monitor now shows a hieroglyphic-like stone carving of an ancient Incan native who appears to be positioned on his back inside some kind of flying capsule. He's staring out a small portal window while operating sophisticated controls with his hands and feet. Then comes another carving of a man who appears to be wearing a modern-day spacesuit which is remarkably reminiscent to the atmospherically independent spacesuits that modern astronauts don today during their space shuttle flights.

I turn back to Keogh.

"So what is it you want from me, Peter?" I say. "Bottom line."

"What I would like from you, Chase, is to follow the path of my father, and to do so on foot."

"Into uncharted Amazonia territory?"

"I want you to team up with my men, Rodney and Carlos, to find the cave he drew for us on this map, and I want you to find the aircraft that is stored inside it. Rodney will be group leader, but once you are in the jungle, they will follow your lead to the site."

"Are you assigning specific tasks to Rodney and Carlos?"

"Rodney is not only a trained Navy Seal but he's flown everything under the sun and then some. If the craft can be flown by a human being then he will be the one to do it. Carlos is a trained videographer. He'll record the entire expedition."

"So that you might show it on cable TV later."

He smiles.

"This is not a commercial expedition, Mr. Baker. If the aircraft is indeed there in the jungle, and we are able to prove its presence, it will be the ultimate piece of evidence that proves not only in the existence of intelligent extraterrestrials who come from inhabited planets located in both ours and distant galaxies, but it will prove our species interacted with them in order to vastly improve their culture, their science, and their overall lives on planet earth." He pauses for a moment while the digital image of his father's map once more appears on the High Def monitor. "It just might also prove something else."

"And what's that, Peter?"

"That humankind evolved not only from monkeys, but also from extraterrestrials."

12

I might have asked Peter Keogh III if I could have a few days to think the idea over. Maybe talk it over with Leslie, get her thoughts on the matter. But I'm already aware of how they'd both respond. The former would tell me he doesn't have long to live and that time is of the essence. He would also plant a fat deposit in my hand which would lead to a much fatter payday, and even a triple fat bonus should I succeed in my quest (fingers crossed).

The latter would tell me that first of all, I need the money, and second of all, the whole thing, if nothing else, will provide me with the idea for a new book.

I can't argue any of these points. It's official: Taking on Peter Keogh III's assignment to locate an ancient aircraft in the uncharted jungles of the Amazon is a no-brainer for a Renaissance man like me.

I retrieve my pistol from the terminal locker while, afterwards, both Carlos and Rodney escort me back to my place on Prince Street.

"Get a good night's sleep," Rodney says while pulling over to the curb in front of my building. He turns to me, grins. "Looking forward to getting some jungle time with you, Chase man. Word up is that you fancy yourself a tough guy." The grin turns into a smile, revealing a solid gold cap that covers a fang-like incisor.

"Can't wait to see if it's the truth or another one of your fictions."

Reaching into his chest pocket he pulls out a business card, hands it to me from across the seatback. I take a quick glance at it. There's no name on it. No physical street address or website address. Just a phone number. I stuff the card into my chest pocket along with the card Carlos gave me earlier.

"Thanks," I say. "I'll call you if I get lonely."

Carlos takes hold of my arm.

"Don't let him worry you," he says, in his soft tone. "As you can see, Rodney likes to show his muscles."

"Muscles are one thing, Carlos," I say with my eyes still locked on Rodney's eyes. "But real strength is an entirely different story altogether."

Opening the door, I get out.

"See you in the morning, gentlemen," I say, sticking my head back inside. "I assume you'll retrieve me at dark thirty?"

"If not sooner," Rodney says.

I close the car door without saying goodbye.

13

My bags are shoved up against the wood door to my second-floor apartment. Maybe it's a relief they've showed up, but what's not a relief is knowing I have just enough time to wash and dry their contents before I have to repack it all, then get some much needed rest.

"Oh well," I say to my three-year-old black pit bull, Lulu, as I fill her food bowl with dry food, "out of the jungle and into the frying pan."

"Jeez, Chase," she says, with a full mouth. "You just freakin' got home. Now I gotta depend on that seedy old Italian pizza maker to feed me twice a day and let me out to poop."

"I thought you liked Vincenzo."

"I do. He plays with me and sometimes brings me pizza crusts … Oops, you weren't supposed to know that … But nothing beats a dog and his master."

"You rock, Lu," I say. "Don't know what I'd do without you."

"And don't forget your baby girl, Chase."

"You don't have to remind me, Lu. But on a good note, she doesn't even know I'm home yet, which means she's not missing me nearly as much as I'm missing her. Soon as I get back, I'll take her upstate for some camping."

"That's a good dad."

I undress down to my boxers and toss everything else in the

small apartment-sized washing machine. While the clothes enter into their first wash cycle, I pull out my laptop and go immediately to the Google search engine.

Typing in the name Peter Keogh III, I come up with over three hundred thousand hits, which tells me Keogh III is a pretty popular guy. As logic would dictate, I click on the first selection. It's the website for Keogh Commodities. The home page shows the exterior of a skyscraper in midtown Manhattan from the point of view of the ground-floor exterior. There's a big American flag that's flying from a metal post which is embedded horizontally into the metal and glass exterior wall. The flag is blowing in the wind on a brilliant sunny day, probably in the early fall. Makes me want to go for a walk and buy some commodities.

My eyes focused on the site's menu, I click onto a page called Bios. Keogh's is the first to come up since he's the commodity commander in chief. The short of it is that he was born in 1939 (the year his father disappeared in the Amazon jungle), educated in a Catholic prep school in Manhattan, then sent off to Providence College in Rhode Island, where he exceeded at rugby and something else: flying. From Providence he went straight to the Air Force Academy and from there Vietnam, where he became an ace, having shot down twenty-two Chinese flown MiGs. At the end of the war, he was decorated for bravery in the skies by then President Johnson, and from there, attended Harvard Business School. Upon graduation he began his commodities firm which, through the years, has amassed enough personal wealth for him to become a serious aviation collector.

Serious as a coronary that is.

From what his bio, and the accompanying full-color digital glossies, clearly indicate, Keogh III just might be in possession of the greatest private aeronautical collection in the world. He owns one of the three Wright brothers Kitty Hawk airplanes ever known to have existed (one is missing, one is housed in the Smithsonian, and the third in Keogh's Oyster Bay Long Island hangar). He also owns a 1917 Fokker DR-1 Triplane like the Red Baron flew, a 1929 Travel Air 4000 biplane, a 1944 North American P- 47G Mustang, a 1944 Fieseler V-1 Buzz Bomb which terrorized London during the Blitz, a 1953 Bell 51C "MASH" chopper, a 1959 Boeing VC-137 Stratoliner, a mid-1970s-era MiG, and even a Gulf War–era Stealth fighter jet, or what's more commonly known in aviation circles as a YF-23 Black Widow II.

I lean back in my chair, attempting to comprehend how much a collection like that might be worth. In my head, I'm not seeing millions of George Washingtons flashing through my brain, but billions. How much is Keogh III paying me to find that ancient airplane for him? I think we forgot to discuss price, which is not entirely untypical for me. That's the reason I'm usually half broke and guys like Keogh are wealthier than the gross national product of some small island nations.

I push down the lid on the laptop and get up. Time to turn over the laundry. But before that, it's time to pop a beer. Heading into the small galley kitchen, I pull a can from the fridge, take it back out to the combination living room/dining room with me, and pop the top.

The first swig has yet to descend the length of my esophagus when I hear the noise coming from the bedroom.

14

Quietly I set the beer can down on my writing table beside my laptop, and then pull the .45 from my jacket pocket.

"Lu," I say aloud, knowing that it's possible the pit bull could be responsible for the noise, but knowing in my gut that she's isn't. After all, Lu's favorite pass time aside from eating is sleeping.

I hear the noise again. It's a short, sharp slap. Like wood against wood, followed by the sound of my mattress creaking, like someone just sat him or herself down on my bed.

Sliding back the cocking mechanism on the .45 so slowly I feel the bullet entering the chamber more than I hear it, I take it lightly over the wood floor to the apartment's compact bedroom. The door is closed, but not entirely. Hiding my body behind the wood door, I try to capture a glimpse into the room through the narrow crack between the door's edge and the wood frame. I see the bed. Rather, not only can I make out the bed, but I can plainly see that someone is lying in the bed, under the covers.

I thrust the door open, hold the pistol barrel onto the figure in the bed.

"Don't move," I say. "Just slowly pull out your hands, and then let me see your face. Do it now."

I see movement coming from under the blanket and sheet. A drop of sweat rolls from my forehead, down my left cheek, where it remains suspended under my chin. For all I know, there will come a shotgun blast from under the blankets and my inside are about to be spattered all over the wall. Too late now.

Suddenly, a hand emerges from under the covers. Then another hand. They are beautiful hands. The hands of a beautiful woman. A head emerges. The head is veiled in shoulder-length brunette hair, and the face is one I recognize well.

I pull back the pistol and thumb on the safety.

"Christ almighty, Leslie," I say. "A text warning me of your arrival might have been nice."

"That would have spoiled the surprise, Chase Baker. Now aren't you glad you've entrusted me with a key?"

I wipe the sweat from my chin with the back of my free hand.

"You scared me half to death."

"I thought the Man in the Yellow Hat doesn't scare so easily."

"It's called grace under pressure."

"Well," she says, pulling off the covers to reveal her entirely naked body. "Are we going to talk? Or are we going to have an adventure together?"

"I choose adventure," I say, jumping onto the bed.

15

Afterwards, we're drinking red wine from the same plain little drinking glasses they use in the Italian restaurant downstairs. Taking my time in order not to skip over any detail, I fill Leslie in on the assignment Keogh III just laid in my lap. When I'm done I pour more wine and ask my agent what she thinks.

"First off," she says, "you were right to take the job. You need it. But you never negotiated a price and that will be my job."

"Thought you were done with agenting."

She cocks her head, flips back her thick hair with her free hand, sips some more wine.

"I've decided to maintain a small list of writers who sell. I'll work from out of my apartment."

"Did I make the cut?" I smile.

"It just so happens you did, Man in the Yellow Hat." Lifting up her right hand, she makes a pinching gesture with her thumb and index finger. "By this much. A smidgeon."

"Wow, I feel blessed."

"You are blessed. Very blessed, and I'll tell you why."

"Okay. Why?"

"Because I'm not only going to remain your ever loyal and superlative agent, I'm going to go you one further."

I'm silent for a minute, wondering just what it is she has up her sleeve. Metaphorically speaking, of course.

"I'm waiting."

She sets her hand on my naked thigh.

"With the gynie not being entirely happy with me now, and me not being entirely happy with him, I'm as free as a bird to do anything and go anywhere I want."

I'm beginning to see where this is going, and because I can see where it's going, I feel my pulse pick up.

"Not a chance," I say. "Not only do we have no idea who we're dealing with in terms of my expedition leaders, Rodney and Carlos, but we're heading into territory that is entirely uncharted, even by today's digital GPS standards. We don't know what we're going to encounter once we get past Machu Picchu and enter into the Amazonian canopy. Plus, there's lots of spiders and snakes and creepy crawler things that girls hate."

She smiles and shoves herself closer to me, as if her skin on my skin will become more of a convincer.

"What's the matter, Chase?" she says. "You afraid I might break a nail?"

"I'm afraid your shrunken head might be used as a charm on some native's necklace."

"You're being dramatic, letting that fiction mind run away with itself. Head hunters are long gone. The natives in the Amazon have smartphones, satellite TV, and Netflix accounts."

"How do you know?"

"I read *National Geographic*." Shrugging her shoulders. "Or look at the pictures anyway."

"That's reassuring."

She drinks down her wine, holds out her glass for more. I fill it.

"Listen," she says, "do you want me to negotiate the right price for this job or what?"

"Sure."

"Then I'm your partner."

"Partner."

"Take it or leave it," she says, slowly slipping her hand from my thigh to another, more sensitive place altogether. "Besides, you owe me. I might not be without an agency if you hadn't set that lit cigar on the edge of the desk of all places."

I take a drink of wine and think about it for a brief second or two. I know my agent. When she gets an idea in her head, not even a hammer drill can pound it out of her.

"I thought you were planning on spending the rest of your years lounging on the beach in the Hamptons."

"Change of plans. I'd rather avoid the Hamptons and all the gynie's rich friends right about now."

"Adventure," I say. "You want adventure."

"Exactly, Mr. Man in the Yellow Hat. On a daily basis I read about adventurers and the faraway places they explore where they fall romantically in love. It's time I experienced some of the real thing."

"Curious George," I say, kissing her on the mouth.

"Curious horny Leslie," she says, rolling her naked body on top of mine.

16

Keogh's men pick us up at precisely five the next morning. As Rodney gets out from behind the wheel of the sedan, his big brown eyes immediately lock on Leslie.

"Who's the dame?" he says, while pulling down on the brim of his blue and white New York Giants baseball cap. He's dressed like a Navy Seal in combat boots, army fatigues, and a tight T-shirt that tells me five sets of bicep curls are far more important to him than sex.

"My agent," I say, stuffing my knapsack into the trunk of the car, which Carlos has opened for me. "She's my partner and she's coming. No negotiation." Hefting Leslie's backpack, I toss it into the trunk beside mine.

Carlos closes the trunk.

"It shall be nice to have a beautiful woman coming along for the ride," he says in that soft, almost effeminate tone of voice. He's wearing a bush jacket and khaki pants that are professionally pressed. For footwear, brand new Timberland hiking boots. For headgear he's wearing a brown, suede fedora that probably cost more than my entire uniform of cargo pants, lace-up jungle boots, and my well-worn bush jacket. Leslie might be a newbie when it comes to jungle trekking, but she knows enough to wear hiking boots over wool socks, tight-fitting cargo shorts, and button-down shirt under a cargo vest that supports a new Canon Rebel camera and two extra zoom lenses. Her headwear consists of a wide-brimmed, oilskin Australian outback hat with a shoestring strap that hangs down under her chin just in case a stiff wind blows.

We pile into the car, Keogh's men up front with Leslie and me in back.

Rodney starts it back up and pulls out.

"She can come with us," he says, speaking to me with his eyes reflected in the rearview mirror. "But she's your responsibility, Baker. You got that?"

"Damn straight," I say.

Carlos turns, smiles.

"This is going to be fun," he says. "In just a matter of hours we will be in the jungle, and soon after that, we will become world famous for locating an aircraft that is a thousand years old. We will turn the history of western civilization onto its back."

"Hold that thought, Carlos," I say. "One step at a time."

Leslie sets her hand on my leg, gives it a squeeze.

"Thanks for letting me tag along," she whispers into my ear.

"I owe you," I whisper back. "Me *and* that damned Cuban cigar."

I set my left hand onto my chest, feel for the .45 shoulder-holstered there. Security in the form of gunmetal, lead, and explosive powder.

"Let's hope you're thanking me later," I say. Then I close my eyes and pray for a quick, preflight nap.

PART II

17

We land in Lima some eight hours later. From there we hop a connecting flight that takes us up to the Sacred Valley. The twin prop plane bounces around the turbulent air of the Andes Mountains like a leaf in a windstorm and it's all I can do to keep our previous in-flight breakfast of microwaved scrambled eggs and bacon from coming up on me.

"My God," Leslie says, as soon as she disembarks from the plane, "I can hardly breathe."

Rodney pulls his sidearm from a pea green military-style holster that also supports a twelve-inch fighting knife.

"That's because you're more than seven thousand feet above sea level." He smiles, clearly the type to enjoy life the more uncomfortable it gets. "That's the equivalent of a mile and a half."

"Shouldn't the air be cooler?" the lit agent turned explorer says, while wiping a bead of sweat from her forehead with a red bandanna she then wraps around her neck, Boy Scout style. Or should I say, Girl Scout.

"It is cool," Carlos chimes in. He's lighting a cigarette with a good old-fashioned Zippo. "You just don't feel it as much because you're in the Amazon jungle. All you feel is the humidity."

"Welcome to the Sacred Valley," Rodney says, "where the only thing sacred is the name." He turns to his left, extends his arm and points. "Over there through that foggy haze is Machu Picchu."

Turning further left. "Over there is the Urubamba Province and the Urubamba River. The road we'll take today will follow the river around the base of Machu Picchu until we come to an entry point into the jungle that our guides have already established for us."

Pulling my .45 from my shoulder holster I thumb the clip release and check the bullet load. When all looks good, I slap the clip back home, make sure the safety is on, and slip it back into my holster.

"Soon as everything is unpacked we'll grab some water," I say to Leslie, as I squeeze a good amount of insecticide onto my palm from a small plastic bottle. "Also, bring along some waterproof matches, some energy bars, and make sure your phone is fully charged just in case you get lost."

I toss her the insecticide.

"Why would I get lost?" she says, snatching the bottle out of mid-air.

Rodney shoots me a grin.

"Come on, people," he barks, "everyone helps unload. The flyboy has other charters to fly today."

With the unloading completed, Rodney assembles us all on the airstrip. Placed on the flat ground behind him are not only our knapsacks, but also the equipment we'll need to carry with us on what we anticipate as a two-day expedition into the jungle. The equipment includes machetes, hand-held GPS direction finders, insecticide, LED flashlights, mosquito netting, tents, sleeping bags, washbasins, cooking equipment, water and water decontamination pills, freeze-dried food, and more. We'll also be carting an impressive assortment of weapons. AR-15s with attached grenade launchers, .9mms for sidearms (I'm sticking to my .45), twelve-inch fighting knives in leather sheaths, assorted explosives, and other destructive treats. We have C4 charges and accompanying detonators should we need to blast our way into the cave where supposedly the aircraft is housed. We also have portable digital film equipment for recording our every step and for which Carlos is in charge.

"You'd think we were starting a small war," Leslie says, folding her arms over her chest.

"The rule of thumb in the jungle," Rodney says, as the sound of a truck entering onto the opposite side of the airfield breaks up the relative quiet, "is never get out of the boat. But since we won't be in a boat, the rule will be, never be caught in a situation you can't shoot your way out of."

"I like the way you think, Rodney," I say. "You would have made an awesome hippie back in the sixties. Peace, love, and understanding."

"Rodney hates hippies," Carlos notes, hefting a video camera up to his face, his right eye now hidden by the viewfinder. "Smile," he says. "You're on Hopelessly Lost in the Jungle Candid Camera."

"Can it, Carlos," I say. "That's bad luck."

"My apologies, fearless leader," he says, lowering the camera.

"Actually Rodney is the fearless leader," I say. "I'm just trail master, and a timid one at that. Isn't that right, Rod the Mod?"

"Okay, everyone," Rodney barks, his dark, round face painted with a sheen of sweat. "Cut the chatter. Our guides have arrived and it's time for our timid trail master to assume the, ummmm, position." Pulling a bag of chewing tobacco from his pocket, he stuffs a pile into his jaw, chews, and spits a wad of black mucus to the ground. "You ready to lead us through the dangerous jungle, Chase?"

"Still glad you came along for the ride?" I say to Leslie out the corner of my mouth.

She turns to me, pulls her camera from her bush vest, snaps a picture of my tight, scruff-covered face.

"I feel like I'm caught up in a testosterone war," she says. "But I wouldn't have missed this for the world. Thank God for fire."

Hope you're still smiling tonight when the spiders and snakes come out, I want to respond, but it's probably better that I keep my mouth shut and start focusing on the job Keogh entrusted me with.

Our team of guides is comprised of four men who are clearly descendants of the ancient Incans. They are short, but stocky, and dressed in baggy-fitting blue jeans, leather boots, and hand-knitted llama wool ponchos. Covering their heads are wool hats shaped like cones and that possess flaps for ear protection as well as fuzzy-tipped tassels. Their faces are as dark as milk chocolate and weathered like old leather, while their eyes are even darker, but at the same time, somehow bright and alive. All four are chewing something that is clearly not gum since every few seconds they spit the remnants of the substance to the ground.

"They chew coca leaves," Carlos says. "For energy and to curb their appetite. Some of these men will hike for a full day without eating, sustaining themselves only with the leaves. You should try it."

"I survived on the stuff back in ninety-five," I say, "when I was unearthing those mummies in the mountains outside Cuzco. I shed ten pounds."

"I could stand to lose five pounds," Leslie laughs. "Where do I get some?"

"You stay away from it," I say. "It's not cocaine, but the drug is derived from the leaf. Tell you what. You can enjoy some coca tea later on. It's better than coffee but safer than chewing the raw leaf all day."

The men disembark from the truck.

"*Vease bien hijos de puta*," says one of the men directly to Rodney. The shorter and older of the three who seems to be the leader.

"*Besas a tu madre con esa boca!*" barks Rodney in response, he being the only member of the team aside from Carlos, fluent in the language. All the men let loose with belly laughs as they begin loading the equipment onto the truck. When the job is done, Rodney hops up into the truck's flatbed, turns to us.

"Okay, people," he says, "the bus is ready to go."

"We're riding in that?" Leslie says.

"This ain't a joyride in Central Park, lady," Rodney shouts, spitting another cheek full of tobacco juice.

Leslie glances at me, rolls her eyes.

"Maybe it's better if I stop offering up my opinions to the support staff," she suggests.

"Maybe it is better," I say, offering her a hand to help her up onto the truck.

As I climb in, I feel the fine hairs on the back of my neck stand at attention. My gut tells me someone's eyes are focused on us. Setting myself down onto the hard flat surface of the truck bed, I turn to peer over my left shoulder. In the distance, I see a Jeep coming up on the landing strip. Two men occupy the military green Jeep.

"Rodney," I say, "let me borrow your binoculars."

"Is the trail master interested in the scenery?" he says, handing them to me.

I place them to my eyes.

Both men are seated in the front of the Jeep. The driver is sporting long black hair and his narrow face is covered with a scraggly black beard. The one in the driver's seat also has long black hair, but he's clean shaven. He's wearing a cowboy hat, and for warmth, a worn Levi's jean jacket. The one in the passenger side wears an olive green baseball cap and a military-style jacket with the sleeves rolled up to the elbows. He's cradling an AK-47 like it's his newborn baby.

The eyes of the two men are focused on us. The fact that they are stopped, however, tells me they are choosing to keep their distance. For now.

"We've attracted an audience, Rodney," I say, handing him back the binocs. "Ballsy of them to reveal themselves out in the open."

"What's your take?" he says, his face having suddenly turned serious. "Curiosity seekers?"

"Bandits?" Carlos poses, while taking a drag on a new cigarette. "Bandits don't care about revealing themselves to anyone. They fear no one."

Stealing a glance at our guides, I try to gauge their reaction to the presence of our new curious new friends. While I'm certain they've taken notice of the Jeep and its occupants, they don't seem frightened or concerned one way or the other. This might be a good thing or a bad thing. Take your pick.

"Could be bandits," I say, once more locking my eyes on the Jeep. But in the back of my head I'm remembering the trouble I had with the Tupac Amaru Rebels the last time I spent time in Peru. Since then, the group has all but disbanded what with the country's introduction of new terrorism laws and military might. But could it be that the group has resurrected itself? I could pose this question to my crew, but maybe it's better that I don't. Why get them worked up for nothing? Sometimes it's what you don't say that matters most. Chase the cautious.

The Incan workers stuff themselves into the front of the truck, start up the engine. The truck bucks, then begins moving forward.

I turn to Leslie. "Last chance to get out and go home."

"Not on your life, Mr. Man in the Yellow Hat. I'm here for the duration, and you're here to get the goods to write a wonderful new book that will make us wealthy beyond our wildest dreams. Maybe then I can get my agency back."

"Not putting too much pressure on me, are you?" I smile, but knowing the dangers that might be lurking about in the jungle, there is little to a smile about.

"You deserve every bit of it," she says.

I was afraid she'd say something like that.

18

The narrow road winds and bends its way around the base of Machu Picchu, the fast-moving, white-capped Urubamba River running parallel to the road almost the entire way. Two hours later the driver turns onto an even narrower dirt road that zigzags its way up a steep mountainside. The dirt road is wet from a recent rain, super slick, and boasts no roadside barriers, wooden or otherwise, to prevent us from dropping off the sheer cliff face that rises rapidly with every foot of ground covered.

Although I say nothing about it, my heart lodges itself in my throat with every tight one-hundred-eighty-degree turn the truck makes up the corkscrew road. The few times I've looked over the side of the flatbed, I haven't witnessed any kind of road at all, but instead, open air. It's no wonder fifty doctors and nurses were killed in this exact area only a few months ago when the bus that was transporting them up the mountain slid off the side and tumbled two-hundred-plus feet down into the riverbed. Better not to think about that right now. Better to think happy thoughts, like those involving a snake-infested jungle that may or may not still house head hunters.

I have to give Leslie credit. She's not saying a word about it, but I know she's scared to death. That is, judging by the way she grips my hand, squeezing it tightly every time the truck negotiates one of the hairpin turns. Carlos senses her discomfort also, because he does something that takes me by complete surprise. Shifting himself in his seat, he takes hold of Leslie's other hand.

"I'm told the Peruvians have a saying," he says. "'When it is time to see God, it is time to go see God. Until that time, however, you must fear nothing. For nothing cannot hurt you.'"

Leslie bites down on her bottom lip.

"Dropping off the cliff could certainly hurt me," she whispers. "Hurt us."

"Ahhh," Carlos exhales. "But the guide operating this truck has been doing so for ages, as did his father before him, and his father before him. The Peruvians have another saying. 'Place your trust in the unknown. It is what makes life interesting.'"

Leslie bites down harder on her lip, until she issues the faintest of laughs. "You making this shit up, Carlos?"

Now it's his turn to giggle. "But it sounds like something a Peruvian would say, does it not?"

By the time we come to a stop inside an area carved out of the thick forest, I've worked up a sweat. The moisture combines with the humid vapor of the rainforest, making my skin feel slick and my clothing damp.

"Okay, everyone," Rodney says, standing up. "This is where we get off."

We're all happy to exit the truck, including Carlos, who only now releases Leslie's hand.

"I told you it would be all right," he says.

Once on the ground, Rodney pulls out his map, lays it out over the hood of the truck. With Carlos on one side and me on the other, he points to our present position with a red Sharpie. He then hands me the pen and without a word, I draw a quick red line to the position where we want to go, based on Keogh's instructions. This isn't rocket science, but someone has to lead the way, and that's where I come in. But judging from the sometimes steep terrain we're sure to encounter, it's not going to be an easy trek.

Rodney insists, "If it's kosher with you, Chase, I'll take lead since I'm not bad with a gun should we run into trouble. You stay close behind. Leslie, you take the position behind him. Carlos, you take up the rear. Agreed?"

"What about the guides?" Leslie inquires.

"They go ahead of us, clearing a path as they go," I inform. "One will stay in the rear and act as an equipment porter. It's likely that the lead men will reach the day's destination point long before we will. Trust me on that. These guys grew up climbing in these forested mountains, barefoot."

"What about bandits and natives?" Carlos asks. "Have the guides showed any concern whatsoever?"

"Rodney," I say, "you're the only one who's been communicating with them. What's your take?"

The black man shrugs his big shoulders while gripping his AR-15.

"No concerns other than asking us to take the usual cautionary measures," he says.

"What are the usual cautionary measures?" Leslie asks.

"If something or someone tries to kill you, try and kill them first." The big man assumes a delighted expression, exposing that gold-capped tooth.

We all chew on that thought for a moment until I say, "Let's move, people, while we have a few more hours of daylight left."

Cocking his weapon, Rodney spits more tobacco juice to the green vegetation-covered floor and begins the trek into the thick Amazonian jungle.

I follow, with Leslie my literary agent on my tail.

19

The forest is dark, damp, and unrelenting in its humidity. The walking is slow and difficult, even with the guides cutting away the thick vegetation that stands in our way. Between the tall tree canopy that blocks out the sun and thick weeds and vines, you can't see more than a few feet in front of you. The feeling is claustrophobic and, although no one will admit it, more than a little frightening.

We move ahead in silence, the packs on our backs as heavy as our not-so-altitude-adjusted breathing. As I walk, I'm reminded of my dad. As a child I'd beg him to take me along on a jobsite he might be working on. Something that required his special talent for digging unusually deep without causing a cave-in.

Once, he allowed me to join him on a special Saturday dig. He was manning the controls on one of his heavy-duty tracked excavators while I looked on mesmerized at the action from a safe distance. The blueprints called for a depth of more than twenty feet in sandy soil. Such a deep dig combined with the precariousness of sandy soil meant that cave-ins would be a major danger. Or so my dad informed me prior to starting the dig.

At one point, the steel teeth on my dad's excavation bucket hit bedrock on an area where bedrock was not expected. Under normal conditions, he would have had one of his men take a look at the obstacle with a pair of binoculars. But this was a Saturday and my dad was the only man from his crew on site.

"I have to head down in the hole, Chase," he told me while wrapping a rope around his waist and tying it off onto one of the cleats on the excavator. I remember feeling my heart enter into my throat as he grabbed hold of a shovel and made the descent into the narrow pit. Knowing that at any moment, the sides might cave in on him, I stood paralyzed with fear. But I said nothing about it. I didn't want to show my fear in front of my dad. I could only trust him for what he was: a magician of a digger.

Minutes passed while he inspected the pit's bottom, stabbing so hard at the rock with the tip of the spade he was producing sparks. He mumbled grumpily about having to blast the rock out, which was something he never anticipated in his original bid. But now he'd have no choice but to do it. To my dad, a contract might be a contract, but a man's word was a man's word, and a man's word was sacred.

"C4 is expensive, goddammit," he groused out loud. Then, "Oops. Sorry, Chase."

I couldn't quite make out his face from where I was standing far too close to the pit's edge, but I knew he had to be smiling. But when he looked up and saw me standing there, he most definitely wasn't smiling. "Get back, Chase," he barked. "It's too dangerous."

Tossing the shovel out of the trench, he tugged on the rope to make it taut and began the climb out. But he wasn't halfway when both sides of the trench began to give way.

I remember seeing the earth caving in on him from the top down. I wanted to scream, but I couldn't. It was as if someone had cut out my voice box. I stood there beside the excavator shivering in fear as the red-brown sand began to pour down on him until no sign of him existed anymore. There was only the rope which was trembling and buzzing like a guitar string wound too tight from bearing the sudden weight of the sand. I shifted my eyes to where it was knotted on the cleat. I knew that if the knot came loose or worse, the rope snapped, my dad would be buried alive.

But then suddenly, through the tears in my eyes I saw a head emerge from the sand, then a pair of shoulders, and finally a torso and legs. Using the strength in his powerful arms, my dad leapt up onto the solid ground, landing on his knees. He coughed and choked for a full minute before he looked up at me with a sand-covered face and said, "Son, don't ever do what I just did. You got that?" Then he laughed and took me in his arms, and held me tightly.

With every step I take into the jungle, I can't help but feel that same anxiety I felt when my dad entered into that deep trench all those years ago. Only difference now is, I don't have a rope to pull myself out should the sides start caving in on us all.

We trek for more than an hour, until something catches my attention underfoot. It might not be entirely noticeable at first, but there's no denying that we are entering onto something that resembles a foot path. It tells me the guides know precisely where they are going. The path can't be more than one foot across in width, but the length seems to go on forever through brush that now is thankfully thinning out with each step we take. Rodney must notice it too because for the first time since we entered into this dark, almost impenetrable jungle, he turns to me.

"Here it is," he whispers. "One of the paths Keogh's father was hired to find."

"My guess is that the natives have been using these paths for hundreds of years as roads between settlements."

"Maybe for hunting too. There are probably thousands of veins that break off into the wilderness. Getting lost must be pretty damn easy."

"Thank God for the guides," I point out.

"Thank God for GPS," he says. "And our fearless literary trailblazer."

"The things I'll do for money," I say.

That's when Rodney stops dead in his tracks.

"What is it?" I say.

"You hear that, Chief?" he says. "Listen."

I watch him as his dark eyes stare off into the thick forest while he tries to make out something that's happening up ahead of him. I hear it then. One of the guides sounds like he's crying. Another is shouting at him, as if ordering the crying man to hold himself together.

"What's happening?" Leslie begs, the fear in her voice as plain as the dew that drips from the thick vines.

"Don't know yet," I forcefully whisper. "Sit tight."

I hear running. I turn and see Carlos coming up on Leslie from behind, his video camera in hand.

"The porter behind me," he says, while sucking breath, "he won't go any further, Chase. My hearing isn't as good as it used to be, but I swear he keeps mumbling something about the great death being upon us. The death in the jungle. He is positively catatonic."

I lean into Rodney.

"Lock and load," I whisper.

Rodney shoulders his AR-15, begins making sweeps with the short black barrel—ten o'clock/three o'clock, ten o'clock/three o'clock. I draw my .45 and thumb the safety off. Carlos shoulders his video camera, begins filming the stillness which isn't exactly still, and the silence which isn't entirely silent.

"Chase," Leslie whispers, "I'm afraid. Maybe this was a bad idea after all."

"Shhh," I say, bringing the index finger on my free hand to my lips. "Don't say a word."

That's when the arrow whips through bush and pierces Carlos's neck.

20

Rodney shoots at will, his thick index finger pumping the trigger of an AR-15 switched on automatic mode. But the high velocity rounds that blast into the surrounding bush are about as effective as spitting in the ocean.

"Hold your fire, Rodney!" I bark. "Hold your damned fire!"

He stops, smoke oozing from his barrel while the drops of damp that drip onto it sizzle from its intense heat. Down on the ground, Carlos is grasping at his neck where the arrow has pierced it, blood oozing out of the wound. Leslie seems to be in shock as she stands beside me, stiff as a statue, her eyes locked on what appears to be a mortally wounded Carlos.

"Hang tight, Carlos," I whisper forcefully, but my gut is telling me that his is a lost cause.

Then it comes. A wave of arrows flying through the bush, some of them embedding into the trees, others cutting into the earth at our feet, a few zipping by our heads.

"Get down!" I order, grabbing Leslie's collar, pulling her down with me. "Get the hell down!"

My .45 in hand, I search for a face or faces to go with the arrows. But all I see are trees and vines. Until a half dozen hostiles emerge from the thick stuff about fifty yards out and sprint directly for us, banzai charge style.

From where I'm positioned I can see that they're dressed only in leather thongs, everything else exposed including their feet. Their hair is long and greased back against their heads while their arms, legs, chests, and faces are tattooed with colorful images. Their bows now slung diagonally over their chests, pouches of arrows slung over their backs, they're coming at us with spears that might pass for state of the art in prehistoric times.

"I got the three on the right," I shout to Rodney.

"I got left," he confirms, sending a blast into his three men, dropping them on the spot.

At the same time, I trigger three shots, aiming from right to left, dropping the remaining three hostiles.

"Sit tight," I insist, as the hot, humid air goes quiet. "There could be another team in reserve waiting to ambush us."

Rodney changes out the clip on his AR-15.

"I need to make a check on the guides," he says.

"Get them up on the radio," I say.

He presses the broadcast button on his chest-mounted walkie-talkie, speaks some Spanish into it. When he releases the button, we both wait for a reply. But all we can make out is dead air.

"Try again," I demand.

He does it.

More dead air.

"Shit."

"What do we do, Chase?" Leslie says, speaking for the first time since the attack began.

I plant my eyes on Carlos. He's no longer struggling to remove the arrow from his neck. His soul has clearly left his body.

"We go back the way we came," I say.

"Not a chance," Rodney says. "Carlos knew the risks. You know the risks. We all *know* the fucking risks. Keogh didn't send us all the way out here to quit at the first sign of trouble."

"Case no one's noticed," I say, "we got a man down."

Propping myself up onto my hands and knees, I crab my way over to the wounded man, press my fingers against his jugular, my left ear over his mouth. Then, lifting my head, I add, "Correction: We've got a very *dead* man down. And now it's possible our guides are dead, or at the very least, run off."

"I'm surprised at you, Chase," Rodney says, as he climbs back up onto his feet. "From what I've heard, you're not the squeamish type. I should think you'd want to find the cave and the aircraft as much as we do. More so, even. Casualties of war or no casualties."

I didn't know we were at war...

He's right and he knows it. I feel my heart beating in my chest, and I feel the sweat that soaks my skin and clothing. But I also smell fresh blood and gunpowder. Turning to Leslie, I place my hand on her shoulder.

"You okay, Agent?" I say. "You want me to lead you out of this death trap, say the word. Rodney might be expedition leader, but he is not my boss."

She assumes a sitting position, brushes the soil from her arms. Swatting a mosquito from her face, she inhales and exhales.

"I live with dead men and dead women in the fiction manuscripts I read every day," she says. "But I've never seen a real man killed before my eyes. One as nice as Carlos anyway."

I instantly recall him pointing a knife at me back in New York, but I quickly dismiss the thought. That was prior to our getting to know one another, so to speak.

Leslie gets up.

"Do you want to leave?" I repeat.

She wipes her face, takes a drink from her water bottle, and exhales profoundly. "This might surprise you. But my vote is to keep going, Chase. Rodney's right. You came here to do a job. Let's keep on doing it. My guess is that Carlos would have wanted it that way. And besides, we have a book to write."

But this expedition is far more than simple research for a new novel. This is about uncovering a relic that, if it's real, will not only turn history onto its back, it will prove once and for all that mankind has not only been the beneficiary of help from ancient aliens, but that humankind is indeed derived from ancient aliens. The enormity of locating the Golden Condor is almost too great to contemplate since it will challenge our everyday notions about God and religion, and it will force us to accept the fact that we are not the isolated species we once thought ourselves to be, and therefore, not the most important life in the universe.

There's no question in my mind about the course of action we must take. And that course is to keep on going no matter what or who stands in our way. The chase for the Golden Condor is why I was put on God's earth. And something else too: if we weren't close to finding it, the hostiles wouldn't be trying to kill us.

I pull myself up onto my feet. "Rodney, call Keogh, tell him what's happened. Let him know we're proceeding as planned. We're going to find the Condor even if we die trying."

"Consider it done," Rodney says, pulling his cell phone out. He walks on ahead of us, his phone pressed against his ear.

"I can't stop shaking," Leslie says, her eyes still locked on Carlos.

I strip the deceased man of his wallet, passport, cash, and cell phone, toss them to the side.

"Come on," I say to Leslie. "Take hold of his feet while I grab his hands."

Working together, we shove the surprisingly heavy, dead-weight body off the path and into a section of thick brush.

"The ground is filled with roots," I say. "It'll be impossible to bury him here."

"The insects will get him," Leslie points out. "So will the animals. In this heat he'll rot away almost immediately."

"Let's at least cover him up."

Pulling his sleeping bag from his pack, I drape it over his body. We then cover the body with leaves and brush. For a brief moment, Leslie and I stand over the mound that conceals Carlos's body.

"Shouldn't we say something?" she says. "You know, like a prayer?"

I catch a quick glimpse of Rodney where he's standing about thirty paces up trail. He's still on the phone. The expression on his face isn't exactly unhappy or anxious. I'm guessing a team member's death doesn't mean a whole lot to the big man. At least, not in terms of the broader picture...the big prize to be uncovered up inside a mountain.

"Rest in peace, Carlos," I say, after a time. "Pleasure sharing a cab ride with you."

"Amen," Leslie whispers.

"Amen," I say.

Retrieving Carlos's AR-15, I hand it to Leslie, who straps it over her shoulder. I grab his passport and the rest of his personals and stuff them into the pockets on my bush jacket. The last item to salvage is his video camera.

"How would you like to do the honors now?" I say, holding out the camera for her. "After all, media is your specialty."

She grabs hold of the camera, fiddles with its buttons and controls like she knows what she's doing. And as a former Columbia film school student, she does.

"Good. It will take my mind off Carlos," she says. Then, while shouldering the camera, "What about the guide who was behind us?"

"He's gone," I say. "My guess is he ran off at the first sign of trouble." But what I'm thinking on the inside is that he's probably as dead as Carlos.

"Wasn't he carrying food?"

"We'll have enough in our packs. After all, we won't need as much now and we're only here for forty-eight hours."

"Let's hope so," she says.

Rodney whistles to get our attention.

Leslie and I turn, focus our eyes on him.

"We got a go from Keogh," he barks.

I nod, knowing full well that the danger we just encountered is not a one-time-only deal.

"Let's go get this thing done and then get the hell out of here," I say. "Keep your eyes and ears open, everyone."

"Open wide," Leslie says, her confidence brewing despite the death that weighs heavy in the air, like the thick jungle humidity.

21

We walk for another two uneventful but tense hours. The path beneath our feet is widening while, at the same time, the tree-lined canopy above our heads is getting taller and thicker, so that what's left of the late afternoon sun is almost completely blocked out, like an unexpected partial eclipse. But then, just like that, the darkness is replaced with bright sunlight as the canopy is suddenly broken by an unexpected opening in the jungle.

Rodney stops, turns.

"You hear that?" he says, his voice soft but strong at the same time.

I stop, listen.

I hear water. Water flowing. Taking another step forward I confirm my suspicion. What lies before me is a deep gorge. At the bottom of the gorge is a high, swift-moving river that's filled with rapids. Leslie stands beside me. Carlos's video camera pressed to her shoulder, she's filming the river.

Rodney adjusts the Giants baseball cap on his head, catcher style, so the brim goes around the back.

"There's our access across the gorge," he says.

A few feet before us is the entry to a long arcing rope bridge, the floor of which is constructed from thin wood panels that, to the naked eye, appear older than my long-deceased grandfather.

Leslie slowly lowers the camera, runs her forearm over her

sweaty brow.

"You want to cross that," she says like a question.

Rodney retrieves his water bottle, takes a deep drink.

"I've seen worse," he says.

"Where?" I say.

The big man replaces his water bottle on his hip.

"I lied," he says. Then, turning to me, his white-knuckled hands holding tightly to his AR-15, "I guess as team trailblazer, you get the honor of going first." Then, grinning, "Age before balls."

"You're one hell of a nice guy, Rodney, you know that?"

"So my mother tells me anyway."

Making my way to the bridge entry, I'm able to look down into a gorge that must be two hundred feet deep. The power of the rapids is so intense, I feel the cool mist of the clean river water rising up into my face, coating it.

"Chase, I've got a lot invested in you," Leslie says. "Be fucking careful."

"Thanks for the kind words," I say. "I think."

Taking hold of the thick ropes on either side of me, I take a step out onto the first, damp-soaked wood plank, distribute maybe half my weight onto it. The slippery plank holds. Swallowing a breath, I take a second shaky step onto the same board. Releasing some of the tension in my arms, I bear almost my entire weight onto the board. That's when I hear a sharp crack, and the bottom drops out from under me.

22

Leslie lets loose with a scream.

Rodney shouts, "Chase, hold on!"

But he doesn't have to tell me twice, as I grip the ropes tightly while flexing my arms to support my entire body weight, preventing my body from falling through the bridge. As luck would have it, only a portion of the first board has split off. Maybe one-third of the entire three-by-one-foot-long piece. If I place my feet on the still intact portion, it seems strong enough to hold me.

Glancing at what's left of my team over my left shoulder, I bark, "Wait until I'm in the center of the bridge. Then you two follow. Leslie, you're next. Rodney, you follow. Wait until she gets to the center before you even think of proceeding. We need even distribution on this thing."

I take another step onto another board. It holds. Then another step and another. The bridge begins to sway and rock with my weight. It feels as though it might capsize entirely, spilling me out into the chasm. But this isn't my first trek across a rope bridge and I know that the sensation of impending doom is mostly psychological.

I wave my right arm over my right shoulder.

"Let's go!" I demand, knowing in my gut that at any moment, a team of hostiles could wage a second attack on us, especially when we're so vulnerable. At least, that's the way I'd do it if I were them.

I don't see Leslie enter onto the bridge so much as I feel her. The new weight distribution on the rope bridge is causing the center to bounce up and down, but not severely so. Leslie can't weigh more than one hundred twenty pounds. It's Rodney I'm more worried about. He easily tips the scales at two hundred twenty-five pounds. In truth, I should make him wait until Leslie and I are safely across, but time is of the essence.

"You okay, Les?" I shout.

"Right behind you, Chase."

"You're not filming, I hope. I just want you to concentrate on your balance." I turn to catch a glimpse of her. I'll be damned if she isn't filming the entire walk across the bridge, while she grips the rope on her left with her free hand. Guess I never realized just how brave my literary agent is. Now I know.

I'm closing in on the opposite side of the bridge as Leslie reaches the very center, where she aims the camera down at her feet in order to shoot the river rapids hundreds of feet below her. What a show that is going to make; that is, if we survive to produce the tale.

"Okay, Rodney, you're next!" I insist, my voice mixing with the roar of the rapids below while echoing off the solid rock gorge walls.

The big man gingerly steps onto the first plank, then the second. He's slowly making his way toward the center of the bridge when a wave of razor-sharp-tipped arrows fly directly for us.

"Holy shit, we're sitting ducks!" Rodney shouts.

He picks up his pace as the arrows shoot past his head.

I turn completely around to eye the opposite bank we just came from, and see another band of hostile natives emerge from the bush, poising themselves before the bridge, combat position. Leslie turns and aims the camera at them in order to get the shot. She's not only brave. She's crazy.

Pulling my pistol from the shoulder holster, I trigger off a burst of rounds that don't connect with flesh and bone, but hopefully will make them think twice about chasing us over the bridge. Another volley of arrows fly, one of them coming so close to Rodney's head, he flinches. But within a second or two I can tell by the trickle of blood that the arrow actually nicked his right ear lobe. Anger gets the best of him. He turns, points his AR-15, fires from the hip. He drops the first hostile on the far right.

The bridge is bobbing up and down.

Leslie is doing all she can to maintain her balance and shoot the action with Carlos's camera. I could easily take the few steps to the safety of the bank, but my gut is telling me to help Leslie.

I don't take two steps in her direction before the board beneath her feet crumbles.

23

Leslie falls but manages to catch herself with both her arms wrapped around the bottom bridge support ropes. The video camera slips out of her hands, dropping down into the gorge where it's swallowed up by the rapidly moving water.

"Chase!" she screams.

"Leslie, don't move!"

Another volley of arrows whips past my head. Rodney shoots at the hostiles again, but what was just a small handful of natives is now turning into an entire army that is not only gathering on the opposite bank, but entering onto the bridge.

"I can't hold them," Rodney shouts.

"Get out of there. Just get the hell off the bridge."

I holster my .45 and arrive to the place where Leslie is hanging. She's supporting herself by having tucked the bottom rope under both armpits, while her feet dangle in mid-air.

"Leslie," I say, holding out my left hand. "You have to take my hand and I will pull you up. Do you understand?"

She nods.

"Am I going to die, Chase? What the hell was I thinking by trying to be Robert Capa when I should have been saving my skin?"

"You're not going to die. Not on my watch, Les. Now grab on."

She goes to lift up her right hand, but the rest of her body slips away. She screams, and once again grabs hold of the rope with both her hands.

"I can't do it," she cries.

I steal a glance at Rodney. He's making his way toward us while the hostiles follow. I know there's no way the bridge is going to support our entire weight, plus the weight of the hostiles. As if to prove it, I see the top rope to my right growing so taut, its individual twines are beginning to unravel. With each up and down and sideways movement of the bridge, another piece of twine snaps and unwinds, further weakening the rope.

"You can do it, Leslie. You have to do it." Once more holding out my left hand. "Now grab hold. I promise I won't let go. You ready? On three."

"On three," she repeats.

"One, two ..."

"Three," she screams, shooting up her left hand, taking hold of mine.

I pull with all my strength. It's as if Leslie weighs nothing at all, as her entire torso emerges from beneath the bridge and then sets itself onto the wood plank that's also supporting my weight.

The plank cracks. I feel the crack more than I hear it. In a matter of seconds, it too is going to disintegrate and send us both to the bottom of the gorge.

Another volley of arrows passes.

Rodney shoots until he can't shoot anymore.

"I'm out!" he yells.

He's running toward us now, the wood planks snapping and breaking beneath him with each thunderous step. He's nearly upon us when, to my right, the top rope begins to rapidly unravel at its weakest point, causing the bridge to begin listing dramatically to the right.

"Chase!" Leslie screams. "We're going over."

"Go!" I shout. "Get to the bank. Crawl on all fours if you have to."

From down on all fours, Leslie speed crabs the final twenty feet to the bank opposite the hostiles. I follow on foot, with Rodney on my tail only a few feet behind me.

"Jump for it!" Rodney cries.

I jump.

He jumps.
The top rope snaps, causing the bridge to capsize.
We all fall down.

24

Rodney lands on top of me, knocking the air out of my lungs. He rolls off of me, his AR-15 still gripped in his hands, miraculously.

"Are we dead?" he says.

"Yes," I say, through gasps of breath, "we're in heaven. Can't you tell?"

I manage to get myself back up onto my feet and go to Leslie. She's standing only a few feet away, her eyes focused on what's left of the now empty bridge.

"All those poor people just fell to their death," she says, through wide, almost shell-shocked eyes.

"You got a problem with that?" Rodney quips. "They were trying to kill us first, in case you hadn't noticed."

"We most definitely do not have a problem with it," I say. "But what I do have a problem with is that it's going to be mighty tough to find a way back across this gorge."

"You'll think of something," Leslie says. "You are the fantastic Man in the Yellow Hat."

Rodney unclips his rifle, stuffs a new clip into the chamber, slaps it home.

"No worries, people," he says, shouldering his weapon. "We're going to be flying out of this place."

I lock eyes onto him.

"You go with that," I say. Then, "Okay, let's mount up and keep going. The light is getting low and we need to find a suitable place to camp before sundown."

Together, the three of us enter back into the jungle. A dark and most hostile place.

25

The jungle is so dark in the late afternoon, we're forced to utilize our LED flashlights to illuminate the narrow path. While Leslie and I grip our flashlights in our respective hands, Rodney uses a headlamp that's been belted above the brim of his baseball cap.

The jungle truly comes alive when the sun dies for the day.

Spider monkeys are hopping from one branch to another, coming close enough to get a good look at us, then scampering off into the leafy cover. All manner of insects crawl up and down the thick trees located on both sides of the trail, while up ahead, Rodney spots a red and black snake, kicking it back into the bush with his boot.

We move slowly, quietly, careful to listen for any further sign of trouble from hostile natives. But a half hour into the mostly level hike, we encounter nothing other than the symphony of sounds created by birds, monkeys, and insects. When we come upon a clearing where the rooftop canopy gives way to the shine of a waxing moon, I know we've found a decent spot to make camp for the night.

What I'm not aware of until Rodney searches the perimeter of the small square-shaped area, is that the guides beat us here already, and died because of it.

I reach out and pull Leslie into me, pressing her face against my chest so that she is blinded to the sight of our three guides who have been stripped naked and nailed to three separate trees by their wrists and ankles. Their tongues have been cut out and their bellies have been sliced open below the bellybutton, their intestines having spilled onto the ground. Red army ants have swarmed, gathering all around the raw, sickly purple and yellow intestines, not only devouring the portion that's on the ground, but also utilizing the hanging pieces of organ as ladders in order to gain access to the tortured men's eviscerated insides.

"Holy Christ," Rodney spits, his voice thick and sick. "I've never seen anything like this in my life. Not even in Iraq. Fucking hostile natives will pay for this. You can count on that."

"This isn't the work of hostile natives," I say, swallowing something dry and bitter. "They're trying to kill us simply because we're trespassing on their territory, simple as that. This here...This is a bit more complicated and it's the work of someone or something else."

"You mean we're not alone out here?" Leslie says. I feel her shivering and trembling against me. Then, "What I mean is, there's other people out here than just a bunch of angry men in leather thongs?"

"What the hell do they want?" Rodney poses.

I shrug my shoulders. "Could be they want the same thing we want."

"But how? No one knows about the aircraft but us."

"You don't know that. But whoever did this knows all about the tortures of war. I used to work with Vietnam vets back in my sandhogging and excavating days. This here ... these men crucified to the trees here ... it's an old trick the Communist North Vietnamese used to great effect to warn American GIs to stay away from their territory. The Cuban revolutionaries under Fidel Castro used the same exact tactic against Batista loyalists. It's their way of warning us to stay away from whatever it is we're going to find up on that jungle mountain."

"You call this a warning?" Rodney says. "I call this cold-blooded murder."

"What did these guides ever do to hurt anybody?" Leslie asks.

"Their only sins are having been in the wrong place at the

wrong time," I say. "The killing is entirely impersonal … a means to an end."

Rodney flashes his light on their faces—on their bloodied, tongue-severed, gaping mouths and at facial skin that was once richly dark, but that now has turned pale white. That's when I can see that the eyes on all three of them are moving.

"Rodney," I swallow. "They're still alive."

Gently, I push Leslie away.

"Turn around," I demand.

"Why? What are you going to do?"

"Just do it, Leslie."

Then, pulling out my .45, I take aim and put a bullet apiece into each of their foreheads.

Things seem to move in slow motion after that, as the sounds of the jungle go silent, and the flash of the discharged bullets burns black holes into our retinas. We just stand there waiting for something to happen. But nothing more can happen, because the guides are now mercifully very dead and very gone. Like a great writer once said, "The dead look so terribly dead when they're dead." These three men are no exception.

"Do we at least cut them down?" Leslie asks, tears running down her face.

"No," I say. "For now we leave them and find another spot to camp, closer to the river. We're exposed and my guess is they're watching us right now."

"You're really going to just leave them?" Rodney asks, a painful tension in his voice.

"They're dead. In the morning we'll come back, cut them down, and give them a proper burial. For now, staying in one place for too long is just too damned dangerous. I just discharged my weapon three times. That in itself is enough of a giveaway, don't you think?"

Rodney bobs his head, runs an open hand up and down his face, as if it's possible to simply wipe away the fear and disgust he is surly feeling. "What about their supplies?"

"Leave it," I say. "We'll survive on what we have in our packs."

He just stands there, looking at me like I'm as evil as the men who truly killed these three guides.

95

"Let's move, Rodney," I say. "I mean it."

"Yes, sir," he barks, brushing past me so hard, I nearly fall to the ground.

Rodney goes silent for the next half hour while we trek on through the black jungle, until we come to another clearing where I decide to make camp for what will surely be a long night of no sleep.

26

With our tents gone, along with our sleeping bags, we have to improvise, which means we'll sleep in our clothing on bare ground made softer by piles of dead leaves and vegetation that we gather up by hand. We make a fire and proceed to boil water in one of the small aluminum cooking pots that Rodney is carrying with him. Once the water is boiled, we pour it into three freeze-dried packets of beef stroganoff.

Sitting around the fire, we eat in silence. Rather, we force our food down.

While I stare into the fire, the events of the day haunt me. I go back to the beginning. Flying into the Sacred Valley, spotting two long-haired men sitting in a Jeep. Men who were armed and observing us as we left the landing strip in the truck. That's when an idea, if not a revelation, hits me.

"Listen," I say, after a time. "The attack by hostiles today might not have been the work of the natives themselves."

Leslie turns to me, her food still resting in her lap, barely touched.

"But we witnessed them attacking us. How could it not have been them?"

"It might have been the work of the Tupac Amaru loyalists who fed a pack of lies to the natives."

"Tupac Ama what?" Leslie says. "I thought Tupac was a rapper who died."

"The original Tupac was an ancient Incan who resisted the Spanish conquistadors led by Pizarro. His name has been borrowed by a group of Peruvian terrorists who backed a communist, Castro-like revolution in the country. Tupac is a band of butchers who will stop at nothing to get what they want. Or, at least, they used to be. They usually make money by kidnapping wealthy tourists and demanding a huge ransom in exchange for his or her release."

"Why doesn't somebody stop them?" Leslie says. "The army? The government?"

"The government did stop them for a while, back in the 1990s. But they've made a resurgence in recent years along with the rise of ecotourism and all those rich, green and sustainable tourists who spend thousands to camp out in the rainforest in order to make themselves feel a hell of lot less guilty about crapping up the environment with their SUVs."

"I've heard of Tupac," Rodney says, after a time. "They live in the jungle. They are always on the move. Never in one place for very long."

"Exactly," I say, "which makes them hard to track. But if they are onto us and our plan to uncover the aircraft, my guess is they will want it as much as we do."

"What the hell would they do with an ancient aircraft?" Rodney asks. "I'm not even sure what we're going to do with the damn thing, if the damn thing is indeed there."

"Now you tell us," Leslie says, making a smirk. "Thought you could fly anything, Rod?"

"Listen," I go on, "a find of that magnitude would solidly place Tupac back on the map as a world terrorist player. The Peruvian government would have no choice but to give in to their demands or else risk losing the one piece of evidence that not only proves the ancients possessed the knowledge of flight, but that intelligent life has existed in the universe for thousands, perhaps millions of years. The entire world would take notice of them. Fear them. Give into them. Obey them."

"Why would they want to kill us if they want the aircraft?" Leslie points out. "Wouldn't they want to let us live long enough for us to find it for them?"

"She's got a point," Rodney says. "We've been fighting for our lives since we stepped into the jungle eight hours ago. It's pretty amazing we're still alive."

I set down the now half-empty bag of beef stroganoff onto the bare earth, stare into the fire.

"Here's my no bullshit assessment: My guess is that we should indeed be dead right now. That whoever is behind the killing, be it Tupac or somebody else, knows enough to let a few of us live."

"That way we lead them to the aircraft," Rodney intuits.

"Exactly," I say.

The big man cocks his head, purses his lips. "Those hostiles sure had me convinced they wanted to put an arrow through my head."

"I'm just giving you an assessment of the situation," I say. "I could be dead wrong."

"Nice choice of words, trailblazer. How will we know if said assessment is correct?"

"If we live through the night, it will be correct. But if we die, I'm wrong." I get up from the ground, brush the soil off my cargo pants, toss what's left of my stroganoff into a plastic garbage bag. "I'll take first watch," I say.

With that, I step away from the fire and into a forbidden darkness.

27

I choose to stand, rather than sit. That way I can be sure of staying awake. Staring out into the eternal darkness of the rainforest, I use my ears more than my vision, which is useless. I can only wonder if I'm being watched by the men responsible for killing Carlos and for crucifying those three guides. My guess is that I am. It confirms my suspicions for me: They need us. Need *me* anyway, to show them the way to the aircraft.

Raising my right hand, I pat the pocket on my bush jacket that contains Keogh II's digitally enhanced map. Without it, I'm a dead man. We're all dead.

Question is, how do the Tupac Amaru know we have such a map? How do they know about our expedition? About the aircraft? How do they know the purpose of our mission in the first place?

The two men sitting in the Jeep earlier...They must be Tupac and what's more, they were waiting for us when we landed this morning in the Sacred Valley. Somebody had to have tipped them off. But who and how? Keogh III doesn't seem the type to take security measures for granted. If the Tupac knew about this mission prior to our arriving, then it had to be an inside job by someone who has no problem with making a deal with the devil. But who exactly? Carlos? Rodney? Carlos is dead, leaving only Rodney. It's possible I could confront him about the situation. But then, maybe the better thing to do is to hold off and let things play out. Either way, I plan on locating that aircraft by tomorrow evening. And when I do, neither Tupac nor any other hostile will get the jump on me, precisely because I will already have texted our precise location to the Peruvian authorities.

I swat a mosquito off the back of my neck. I listen to the constant hum and buzz of the insects foraging for food. The jungle is a loud place at night. A very alive and dangerous place. But that doesn't mean I'm not beginning to feel the onset of exhaustion. Even standing, I feel my eyelids growing heavy.

Until a loud shriek rips through the jungle.

Sprinting back through the thick vegetation, the branches and twigs slapping at the exposed skin on my forearms and on my face, I see the light of the campfire through breaks in the trees and head right for it. When I come to the small clearing I come to a dead stop. It takes me a moment to comprehend what I'm seeing. It looks like a scene from out of a cheap horror movie from the 1950s. But it's not a scene from a horror movie.

It's real.

The dozens of black tarantulas that are converging upon the clearing and surrounding both Leslie and Rodney are all too real.

28

Leslie and Rodney are pressed up against the fire as far as they can go without setting themselves ablaze. They are facing an army of tarantulas as it begins to encroach on every bit of open space in the clearing.

"Stay still, guys," I say softly from the clearing perimeter. "Rodney, take hold of one of the logs that's not burning entirely. Toss it onto the spiders."

Rodney looks at me wide eyed, then turns, staring down into the fire. Slowly bending at the knees, he finds a log, grabs hold of an end that's not burning, tosses it onto the swarm at his feet. The spiders immediately retreat, forming a wide circle around the burning log.

"Now Rodney," I say, "can you find another one?"

Turning, he once again examines the fire. When he's found a log or a stick that looks promising, he reaches down for it, tosses it out a further distance from the first log. Once more the spiders retreat, forming a large open circle around the small torch-like flame.

"Now, I want you two to carefully step away from the fire," I say. "Use the smaller fires to get free of the clearing. Understand?"

"Roger that," Rodney confirms. He takes hold of Leslie's arm and pulls. But she won't move. Her eyes are fixed on the hairy black tarantulas, on their never-ending movement, the way their eight legs are able to make them scatter about rapidly in all directions, as if at any moment they will run up her legs, dig their fangs into her skin and flesh.

"Leslie," I go on, "close your eyes. Don't look at the spiders. Just take Rodney's lead and go where he goes."

She doesn't say anything. She's paralyzed. Catatonic.

"Leslie," I say as calmly, but firmly, as possible. "You need to get out of there before you get bitten. You need to trust Rodney."

"Come on, Leslie," Rodney says, his voice barely a whisper. "Let's go."

He pulls her along onto the first clear ring. Drags her, is more like it. The literary agent issues a cry and goes stone stiff and still.

"You have to keep moving, Leslie," I insist. "Only a few more steps and you're clear."

But to her those few steps must seem like miles and miles.

Rodney shoots me a look, which I interpret as *We don't move now, we're going to be covered in killer spiders in a matter of seconds.*

The second log set a few feet before him is losing its flame. It's about to go out, and to prove it, the spiders are once more closing in on the area. That's when Rodney decides to take matters into his own hands, literally. Reaching out for Leslie, he takes her into his arms, lifting her up and folding her over his shoulder in a classic fireman's hold. He then leaps his way out of the spider trap and to the safety of the jungle.

He comes to me, Leslie folded over his back, not making a sound.

"I should have thought of that sooner," he says, gently letting her down.

"But you don't like spiders any more than she does, do you?"

He shakes his head. "They creep me out."

"Me too," I say. "Give me snakes any day."

"Bite your tongue, trailblazer," he says. "What in God's name do you think is happening here? How could all these spiders exist much less take over the clearing?"

"My guess is they were reclaiming what was theirs to begin with."

"How's that?"

Grabbing my LED lamp off my belt, I flick it on and shine the light up into the trees. That's when we see it plain as day, only under the cover of night, when all the nocturnal forms of life in the rainforest do their eating and killing.

A spider web.

But this isn't the garden variety spider web you find wrapped around the flowers in your backyard garden. This is an almost solid canopy of white silk that itself is filled with hundreds or perhaps thousands of tarantulas both large and small.

"Oh dear God," Rodney swallows. "We camped inside a spider's nest."

"There you have the problem with making camp inside tropical rainforest at night," I whisper. Then, "Lady and gentleman, back away slowly."

With Rodney once more lifting Leslie up and placing her over his shoulder, we back away from the giant spider nest and head back out to the trail.

29

"Now what?" Rodney says, setting a still wide-eyed and very quiet Leslie down onto her feet.

"We find a place to rest our heads for the few more hours until dawn," I say. "Then, at first light, when the spiders are all snuggled back into their silk bed for the day, we'll grab our gear and make our way to the mountain that houses the aircraft."

Rodney takes a look around.

"Where exactly do you propose we lie down in a place that's positively crawling?" Leslie asks, her voice cracking with fear.

I look over one shoulder, then another.

Darkness all around.

Making a 365-degree sweep with the LED lamp, I spot an ironwood tree. It's one of the biggest, oldest, and most rugged trees of the jungle. Thus its name. It also rarely houses army ants, which can be even more deadly in the rainforest than spiders and snakes.

"I think I've just found us a bed," I say, shining the light on the tree.

Together we head the fifteen feet off-trail into the woods. There's several thick branches jutting out from the massive old trunk. Leaping off my feet, I manage to grab onto the branch and, shinning myself up, I swing my right leg up and over the branch.

"Leslie, you're next."

I lower my hand, and she grabs onto it. I pull her up, just far enough for her to swing her behind onto the branch. "Rodney?"

"No thanks, Chief," he says. "Got me my own branch." He grabs hold of the branch on the other side of the tree and hefts himself up like he's doing a pull-up. But instead of making himself comfortable on the branch, he drops back down to the jungle floor. "But I can't even think of sleep after the attack of the killer tarantulas. Tell you what, I'll establish a perimeter twenty or so feet out from this tree and take the first watch. You two get some sleep."

And with that, I watch big Rodney disappear into the thick forest.

Leslie and I scoot ourselves back against the tree. The old branch is so thick, we have room to spare, even with our sitting beside one another. With Rodney being entirely out of sight and sound, it's as if we have our own room inside a five-star tree-hotel, even if the bed is a bit on the hard side.

After a minute or two has passed, Leslie takes hold of my hand, squeezes it. She turns to me. "Thanks for taking care of me back there. It's not like I thought I was going to die. It's more like I *wanted* to die before those spiders started crawling all over me, biting me."

"I feel your pain," I say, running my hand through her thick hair. "We're safe here. For now."

"For now," she whispers, moving her hand from my hand to someplace else entirely. She begins undoing my belt buckle, then she unbuttons my pants. She pulls me out. I'm as hard as this ironwood tree. Harder. Unbuttoning her shorts, she gently pushes them down to her ankles. Then, climbing over me, she takes hold of me and guides me into her. Suddenly all the death of the day and the dangers of the jungle in the night disappear and I am all alone in the world with Leslie. When I come to that place and she does too, we let ourselves go without making so much as a whimper.

Later on, she pulls her shorts back up and snuggles into me. I run my hands through her hair.

"Leslie," I whisper, "I'm glad you're with me."

"Let's go to sleep. You saved my life today. I wanted you to know how thankful I am by giving us both a happy ending to remember."

"I hope to save your life at least twice tomorrow," I say.

She slaps my hand and together we quietly laugh. Soon I feel her breathing become rhythmic, her chest rising and lowering with her every gentle breath. Leaning back against the tree, I look out onto the darkness and think about my words to Leslie ... about saving her life tomorrow, and how prophetic they are likely to be.

As sleep takes over, I find myself very far away from the Amazon jungle. I am suddenly standing inside a four-walled sacristy in a most holy cathedral in Turin, Italy. The cathedral is holy because of the sacred relic it houses. The Holy Shroud of Turin. The burial cloth used to wrap Jesus's body immediately after he was removed from the cross. The linen that bears the blood-soaked wounds on the wrists and ankles where nails the size of spikes pierced them. The cloth that soaked up the blood from the crown of thorns that was pushed so far down onto Christ's head the pincers scraped the bone of the skull. The cloth that bore witness to the blood and pain of forty lashes from a cat-o-nine-tails, and that when viewed from the perspective of a camera negative, shows up as an almost three-dimensional portrait of Christ the Man. This is the Jesus I am staring at where he is horizontally hung from the sacristy wall.

Something happens then.

The Shroud begins to move, tremble, as it takes shape and the image of a man appears. A live man. That man, Jesus, emerges from the Shroud, turns himself upright, and floats down to the floor so that he is standing before me, his many wounds still bleeding, water and blood dripping from the spear wound inflicted by the Roman soldier, Longinus, on his lower right side.

All oxygen exits my lungs like the wind from a sail. I collapse to my knees, my two hands clasped together as if in prayer. He comes closer to me, holds out his hand, exposing a bleeding hole in his wrist.

"Do you believe in me?" he asks in his native Aramaic. I don't know the language, but somehow I understand his words precisely.

"I don't know," I say.

Reaching out, he touches my mouth with his hand, his blood painting my lips. He then takes hold of my hand and clasps my index finger with the two fingers on his hand. He forces my index

107

finger through the hole in his wrist.

"I died for you," he says. "And you found me two thousand years later."

"Yes," I say, feeling the warmth from his flesh and blood wrapped around my finger. "I found your bones. I wrote a novel about it. It's called The Shroud Key.*"*

"Did you believe in me then? When you saw my bones?"

"I don't know," I say, as tears begin to stream down my face. "Your body disappeared...again."

He takes hold of my wrist, yanks my finger out of his nail hole. "He who believeth in me shall have eternal life."

"I want to believe," I say. "I really do want to believe in you. But who are you? Are you human? Are you born of this earth? Or somewhere else entirely? Somewhere way out there?"

"The mysteries of life are many. The clues are few. You and your species are not alien creatures, but then you are not all man either. The power of God is far greater than man. The power of the universe is far greater than God."

"If I'm not all man, then who am I?"

"We have left behind many clues for you to understand your beginning. None of them have convinced everyone of the existence of God. None of them have convinced you of the existence of other worlds. Worlds teaming with life."

"Are you God?"

"I am your maker, and I come from a place far away from here."

That's when something miraculous happens. The blood disappears from his body, as if it were being soaked up by a sponge. His wounds heal, and his body takes on a new shape and color altogether. His body shrinks, his head becomes more ovular, his hair and beard retracting back into the skull and face, his deep brown eyes turning big, black, and egg-shaped. His arms and legs lose most of their mass until they become gray skin and bone. A light emerges from behind him where the sacristy wall was. The light is brighter than the sun. This man, this God, this creature from another world ... he turns and disappears into the brilliant light.

30

Morning comes gently with the newly risen sun breaking through the leafy canopy in sharply angled, if not brilliant radiant rays. It's like the filtered sunlight that pours through the stained glass in a cathedral.

As I clear the sleep from my eyes, I can see that Leslie and I are not alone on the branch. There's something moving around at my feet. But then, moving isn't the right word. Slithering is more like it.

Acting on instinct, my entire body goes stone still. So still I can hear my own heart beating in rhythm with Leslie's heart. She's still asleep, her head resting peacefully on my chest. The snake that is corkscrewing itself around the branch is an anaconda. Its skin is brown and accented with dark-brown, circular and egg-shaped spots. While it's impossible for me to get an idea of its length, I can see that its girth must measure a foot to a foot and a half around.

My mouth goes dry and my pulse begins to pound as the head of the anaconda pops up not by my feet, but over my chest and Leslie's back. Two long, crescent moon–shaped fangs stare me in the face along with two black eyes that clearly recognize their next meal.

I try and reach for my .45 but Leslie's right shoulder is pressed against my chest, dead weight, making it impossible for me to reach for it without waking her and possibly knocking her off the tree.

"Rodney," I say, voice even, non-alarming, knowing that at any moment those fangs could impale themselves into Leslie's or my neck. "Rodney, you hear me?"

"I see it," he says from behind the tree trunk where he's nested himself on one of the thick branches. "Stay still, Chief. Don't move a muscle."

The snake is now wrapping its fifteen- or twenty-foot-long body around both the branch and our legs, while its white-fanged head is slowly inching its way toward my face.

"Rodney," I whisper, as loudly and forcefully as I can. "We're in serious trouble here."

"Stay still. Don't speak."

Then, two fangs, exposed only inches away from my face, the snake's mouth opening wide, so wide I can smell a sweet but sickly sour breath coming from inside its long, dark guts. Until a shot rings out and the anaconda enters into a kind of suspended animation, neither moving toward me nor moving away from me. Leslie pops her head up, focuses tired eyes in the direction of our booted feet. It takes her a second or two to realize what's got itself wrapped around our legs, but when she does, she releases a scream that sends flocks of birds shooting out of their treetop perches.

The anaconda drops its head onto our torsos before its body uncoils itself from our legs and the branch, and drops down hard onto the jungle floor.

Leslie shoots up.

"What the hell was that?" she barks. "Wait! Don't answer. Don't fucking answer. I know precisely what that was."

Her body is shivering, trembling.

Rodney jumps down from his tree branch, stares up at us with a face full of smiles, like we're about to embark on a Sunday-Funday outing in Winnie the Pooh's Hundred Acre Wood. Gripped in both his hands is his AR-15. A slim stream of white gun smoke is rising up from the barrel tip.

"You gonna live, Chief?" he asks.

"I hope so. Help me with getting Leslie down."

He does it. I jump down, land solidly on both feet.

Leslie stares down at the massive dead snake.

"Can I change the channel on my world right now?"

"You're in for the long haul, Les," I say. "Told you you should have stayed in New York. You and the gynie might have made up by now."

She shakes her head.

"How about some breakfast?" Rodney suggests, pulling his fighting knife from his belt sheath. "Anaconda is good eatin' roasted over a campfire."

"I suppose it tastes like chicken," Leslie says. "But no thanks. I've just become a vegetarian."

I look at my watch. It's half past six in the morning.

"It's getting late," I say. "Let's grab the packs and get going. We can eat some power bars along the way."

"Great," Rodney says. "Back into the spider nest."

"Let's hope they're all asleep by now," I say.

"Stop the world," Leslie says. "I wanna get the hell off."

31

The clearing beneath the goliath tarantula nest is entirely devoid of spiders, the black arachnids having climbed back up into their silk beds for the duration of the day, just like I predicted they would.

"Let's get the packs back out to the trail where we'll shake them down," I say. "Make sure no surprises await us on the inside."

I grab hold of both my and Leslie's pack, which I carry out through the bush to the path. When I get there, I open both packs and give them a violent shake. Nothing crawls out. Reaching inside, I move the clothes and food packs around. No spiders. Is it foolish for me to be sticking my hand into a pack knowing a spider bite could very well await me? Maybe. But what most people don't realize is the bite from a tarantula, even a goliath dinner plate–sized tarantula which is common for the Amazon jungle, isn't any worse than the sting of a hornet. But that doesn't mean I'm looking to get bitten. Had all those spiders converged on both Rodney and Leslie last night, their collective bites and the resulting shock might have killed them both on the spot.

"Saddle up, everyone," I say, pulling the Keogh II map from my pocket, unfolding it.

I glance down at our relative position. If we follow the trail as it's depicted on the map in Keogh's handwriting, I'm guessing we'll be spending another full night in the jungle.

But you're not prepared to spend another night in the jungle. Your guides are dead. Most of the food is gone. So is most of the ammo. Not only is the Tupac Amaru after you, but so are hostile natives, and who knows what else. The best solution is to find a faster route to the mountain that houses the aircraft, and once you get there, call in precise coordinates for assistance.

Staring down at the map, I can see that it might be possible to bushwhack our way through the jungle and reach the base of the mountain a half day sooner than expected. But we'll be taking a chance since no one can possibly predict how thick the vegetation is going to be. It's exactly how I put it to Rodney who, with his AR-15 shouldered, his pack on his back, his Giants baseball cap pulled down over his brow, and his machete in hand, is calmly awaiting my instructions.

He cocks his head.

"I see your point in bushwhacking, Chief," he says, his eyes also locked on the map, tracing his way along the jagged line with his index finger. "We can cut the distance between us and our end goal in half if we head on through the bush in this direction." He pulls his eyes off the map, focusing on me. "But two things bother me about this approach."

"Speak freely, Rod."

"Well, first off, that trail was carved out of this jungle floor where it was carved out of this jungle floor for a reason. Meaning that to begin carving another one in another place might lead us head on into a situation we would rather not find ourselves in."

"Duly noted. And second?"

"And second, the jungle is liable to be so thick and unnavigable that it could take us twice as long to get to the mountain than it would if we used the trail."

"Again, duly noted. How about this idea? We bushwhack for a while. Maybe an hour or so. If it proves impossible to get through all that vegetation, then we double back, jump back onto the trail. That way we're only an hour and a half or so behind the original schedule."

Rodney looks at me, nods.

"Good," I say. "Try Keogh Three again, give him a report on the guides, and then tell him about our change of travel plans."

Rodney pulls out his phone, starts dialing. After a time, he shakes his head.

"No answer." He replaces the phone in his pocket, pulls out his radio, makes a call for Keogh III. But all he gets is dead air. "Nothing again."

I don't like the sound of that dead air. Keogh III should be available to us at all times. But for some reason, he's nowhere to be found. A vision of the sickly man sitting in that leather chair hooked up to those many intravenous lines shoots through my overstressed brain, and it dawns on me that he might suddenly be dead. But I decide to say nothing about my vision to my partners. After all, if Keogh III has indeed died, someone on his support staff would have the decency to contact us about it.

"Send him an email and a text," I command.

"What will I say?" Rodney inquires.

"Make it short and sweet. Something like 'Guides dead, taking new route to destination. Make contact ASAP.'"

"That'll do it," Rodney says, thumbing away at the little digital keyboard on his phone.

"Leslie, you okay?" I say, turning to her as she combs back her long dark hair with the open fingers on her hand and repositioning her hat on her head.

I reach out with the palm of my hand to touch her pink cheek.

"You good to go?" I say, touching warm skin.

"I'm ready," she states with confidence. Smiling, she wipes the perspiration from her face with the back of her hand.

"You okay with cutting our jungle visit short?" I pose.

"I'm okay with the new plan," she says, her voice sounding weaker and softer than usual. "Just so long as it means we don't have to spend another night in this place. I've had enough spiders and snakes to last a lifetime."

I re-pocket the map.

"It's settled then," I say. "Rodney, you okay with taking first machete duty?"

"Your wish is my command, trailblazer," the big man says with a laugh.

"Lead the way," I say.

Together, we enter into uncharted territory.

32

You know what they say, Chase. Never get out of the boat. But in this case, you never go off the trail. There's a reason for rules of the jungle, both written and passed down via tribal legend. You value your skin at all, you don't veer from the established path.

But then, you don't have a choice other than to give bushwhacking a try. Your team has been decimated by hostiles. You're down to bare bones supplies. And you can't reach your employer via cell phone or radio.

Plus there's another reason for shortening the time in the jungle.

If the Tupac Amaru is on to you and your quest, they will make it a priority to kill you once you've succeeded in locating the Condor. But if you can get to it first without them knowing, you stand at least a chance of escaping the jungle with both the prize and your lives.

That means bushwhacking...

Providence must be looking down upon us.

Because thus far, Rodney hasn't had to use his machete for cutting much of anything. The layout of this uncharted forest isn't all that different from a pine forest back in upstate New York or central Italy. The trees are so old, thick, and tall that their thick leafy branches are located far above the jungle floor, making walking fairly easy.

We proceed uphill, but not a drastic uphill, the angle of ascent manageable without becoming too exhausting. Out the corner of my eye I keep a constant vigil on both Leslie and Rodney not only to make certain they're both keeping up with the pace, but also to make sure no one is suffering from exhaustion or illness. Out here in the jungle it might be warm and humid, but hypothermia can kick in when you least expect it. So can jungle fevers like malaria and dysentery. The chances of our acquiring both just doubled with our hiking off-trail.

After an hour, I shout out for Rodney to stop.

"Water break," I say. "That includes you, Les."

She pulls the bottle off her belt, unscrews the cap and drinks.

Rodney does the same.

"Going's easy," he says.

Digging into my pack, I pull out a small bottle containing big green capsules. Popping the top, I drop three into the palm of my hand, two of which I offer up to Leslie and Rodney.

"What's this?" my agent asks.

"Malarone," Rodney answers in my stead.

"For malaria," I say. "It's a preventive medicine, so take it."

Leslie swallows the capsule along with a gulp of water, and Rodney does the same.

I check my watch. "It's been an hour. What are your thoughts, Rod?"

"Ain't my call," he says. "You the trailblazer."

I pull out the map, unfold it, press the tip of my finger against what I assume is our location. Pulling out my GPS device, I match up the coordinates on the device to our exact position on the map. The bushwhacking is proving more expeditious than I thought. We keep proceeding like this, we'll make the mountain in less than two more hours rather than having spent all day taking the safe but circuitous route.

I pocket the GPS and put away the map.

"Let's keep going," I say.

We don't get ten more feet before we stumble upon the severed heads.

33

They are the heads of the guides we discovered crucified last evening.

They've been set side by side directly before us in a way that tells me we're not only being watched from our front, but we're also being followed. How else would they know enough to plant the heads here way off-trail?

"Nobody move," I say, my eyes going from the heads to making a one-hundred-eighty-degree sweep of the vicinity.

"Fucking animals," Rodney says, shouldering his AR-15. "Fucking...animals."

"How can anyone be so evil?" Leslie poses, her voice cracking under the strain of her fear.

Silence ensues so that the only noise is the sound of insects flying past our ears and the occasional calls from a Macau or a spider monkey jumping from branch to branch far overhead.

But after a minute of standing still as a statue, I begin to make out something else.

So does Rodney.

"You hear that?" he says.

"I hear it," I say, slowly drawing my automatic, cocking a round into the chamber.

The sound that is filling my ears sounds almost like a stampede. Only not of hooves, but of human feet.

"Christ," Rodney says. "It's another war party."

"Hold your fire and get down," I demand, pulling Leslie down beside me by her belt buckle.

The sound of footsteps trampling through the woods is getting louder. Now it's accompanied by shrieks. Rodney aims his weapon at the source of the noise.

"Hold your fire," I repeat. "Those aren't war cries, Rodney. Those are cries of fear."

He holds his fire.

That's when we see the first man. He's running not at us, but toward us. Another native follows him and another one after that. Soon a half dozen nearly naked unarmed men sprint right on past us, screaming their lungs out.

When they're gone, we rise back up onto our feet.

"What the hell was that?" Leslie says.

"They're afraid of something," I say. "Something out there in the jungle."

"They are afraid of what you came here to find," says the voice of a man who pops his head out of the bush. "The aircraft that you are going to find for us."

The mechanical gunmetal on gunmetal sound of two AK-47s being cocked follows as two rebels emerge from out of the jungle.

They are the men I originally spotted at the landing strip in the Sacred Valley. The men who, no doubt, are responsible for crucifying and now beheading our guides. They approach us with their AK-47s held at the hip, at the ready.

"Your weapons, gentlemen," says the lead man in a heavily accented voice. He's tall, thin, wearing worn jeans, cowboy boots, and a jean jacket over a worn work shirt. He's got a straw cowboy hat that's seen better days planted over a head of stringy black hair while his face sports a matching beard that doesn't know if it's coming or going.

He makes his way to Leslie, reaches out with his free hand, runs it under her felt hat, flipping it off her head. The hat falls down against her back, its string catching on her neck. From where I'm standing, I can see her eyes go wide as he caresses her hair. I see her body go stiff and cold.

The other man is shorter, chubbier. He's wearing military

clothing. Combat boots, green fatigues, and matching jacket, with an olive green baseball hat to match. He's clean shaven, and beneath his chin he sports a bright red bandanna that, if I remember correctly, represents the official color of their terrorist organization.

"Weapons!" he shouts. "Or the woman's brain becomes home to a bullet."

Rodney and I toss a glance at one another. Reaching into my bush jacket, I slowly draw my piece by its barrel so that the grip faces the bandits.

"Drop it," says Military Man.

I drop it.

"You too," he insists, dark eyes now focused on Rodney.

Rodney slowly pulls the AR-15 off his shoulder, drops it at his feet.

"Fuck you," the angry big man whispers.

"Excuse me, gringo?" Military Man barks, shouldering his AK-47, aiming the barrel for Rodney's head, point-blank.

Rodney raises his hands in surrender.

"I said ahhhcchooo," he smiles. "All this vegetation makes me sneeze, compadre."

"I am not your compadre, gringo," Military Man hisses, as he gathers up our weapons while maintaining his lethal aim on both Rodney and myself. Obviously, he's a pro at this sort of thing.

As Military Man backs away, Long Hair removes his hand from Leslie's hair and steps toward me.

"You are the leader, huh?" he says in a deep, throaty voice.

"The buck stops here, asshole," I say, not without a grin.

"Such language," he says, inverting his weapon so that the wood stock faces me. "You should learn better manners. Your life may depend upon it."

When he jams the stock into my stomach, I double over from the sharp abdominal pain and from the sudden loss of air in my lungs. But I don't drop to my knees. Chase the proud and the strong.

It's a struggle, but I manage to straighten myself slowly back up.

"Chase, say something," Leslie says, panic painting her voice. "Are you okay?"

"Silence, *perra*," shouts Long Hair while shooting Leslie a look. Then, turning back to me, "We will make a deal now, Chase Baker."

"You know my name?"

"Yes, I know all about you. You are quite the famous Renaissance man, are you not?"

I force myself to grin, despite an abdomen screaming with pain. "Thanks...I try."

He taps his temple with his index finger. "But you are not always so smart. People in organizations talk, and my hearing is perfect."

"You saying there's a mole in my boss's organization?" Rodney chimes in.

Long Hair turns to the big man.

"Let's just say your Mr. Keogh could use a security upgrade. But enough of this useless small talk. We all want the same thing and you're going to lead me to it."

I could play dumb here and pretend I don't know what Long Hair and Military Man want, but that would only make them more pissed off. And pissing off revolutionary terrorists who are holding locked and loaded AK-47s is probably not the best idea in the world.

"You have a map?" Long Hair poses.

I nod.

"Sure, I've got a map. It's right here in my chest pocket."

"Fuck you doing?" Rodney whispers in my direction.

"Trust me," I say. Then, to Long Hair. "Would you like to see it?"

"Yes," he says, "I would."

Lowering my left hand, I pull the map out and toss it at his feet. Keeping his eyes on me, he squats, picks the map up, unfolding it with one hand. When he glances down at it, his eyes light up.

"This is it, Juan," he cries. "This is the way to the aircraft. In a matter of hours, the world will stand still in shock over our discovery, and they will fear us."

"Now that we have the map, Pedro," Juan/Military Man says, "shall we shoot the gringos?"

"Bad idea," I say.

"Why is it a bad idea?" Pedro giggles. "You are worthless to me now."

"The map doesn't tell you everything."

He squints at me. "How do you mean, everything?"

"What isn't written down are the many booby traps and obstacles that will not only prevent you from entering into the cave more than ten feet, they will terminate your life in a most painful way. Trust me, I did my research."

"You are bluffing, of course."

"Okay, I'm bluffing. Go ahead. Take your chances."

Rodney lowers his hands.

"Hey, you need someone to fly the damned thing, right?" he says.

The long-haired Pedro shoots a glance at Military Man Juan.

"*¿Qué te parece?*" he says. "What do you think?"

Stepping up to Leslie, rubbing her back with his hand, Juan says, "They lead us to the aircraft. We keep them alive for as long as we need them." He grins, revealing brown, crooked teeth. "That includes this luscious little lady. She will come in handy later on when we enjoy a drink or two, and a smoke."

Leslie locks eyes on me. I wink at her like, *Try not to worry.*

"Okay then," Pedro shouts, while waving the barrel of his weapon at us. "The big negro man cuts away the vegetation while you and the *perra* follow. Understand?"

"I understand," I say.

"*Vamos!*" demands the revolutionary.

Prisoners of the unknown, we walk.

34

The hiking is getting harder, the angle of the climb steeper. The vegetation is also getting thicker so that the machete-swinging Rodney is soaked with sweat after only an hour of bushwhacking. I try to get a look at Leslie, who is walking so close behind me, I can almost feel her hot breath on my neck. I know she needs water. We all need water. But the bandits want nothing to do with keeping us hydrated. They want us to show them the way to the mountain, but also they want to keep us as weak as possible. It's standard operating procedure for a revolutionary band like Tupac, just as it was for Castro's bandits many decades ago.

I always chuckle to myself when I see some kid walking the streets of Manhattan or Florence wearing a mayday-red T-shirt that bears the black-stenciled image of a beret-wearing Che Guevara, the bearded revolutionary's black eyes poised upwards at the heavens. These days *The Motorcycle Diaries* author is supposed to be cool, but what most people don't know is the former medical student's penchant for torturing his prisoners and bleeding them to near death in order to build up his own blood bank. Revolution is a bloody business. Che could have told you all about it. So could Pedro and Juan.

I can't see them exactly, but I sense them behind me. Sense their guns. They're laughing, and speaking rapidly in Spanish so that it's difficult for me to understand. I'm somewhat fluent in

Italian since I spend almost half my time in Florence, and the language is not all that different from Spanish. But when it is spoken too quickly, I am easily lost.

One thing I know for sure, however: If Rodney, Leslie, and I can stay healthy long enough, I will find a way to kill these men. Exactly how remains a mystery. But this is the jungle and the jungle poses many dangers. The key will be to capitalize on just one of them.

We walk for another hour.

"I need to stop," Leslie whispers from behind. "I can't go on."

"Are you sure?" I say, surprised to find my own voice a hoarse whisper.

Rodney must be able to make out our conversation, because he stops swinging at the vegetation, which earns him the ire of long-haired Pedro.

"Hey you, *stupido!*" the rebel shouts, running uphill toward us with his AK-47 out front. "Why you stop?"

"We need rest and water," Rodney says, his hand clutching the machete, the long metallic blade bouncing gently off his khaki-covered knee.

"He's right," I say, feeling the sweat pouring off my body. "We need water. Especially the woman."

Military Man Juan comes up on us.

"We keep moving," he insists. "No stopping."

"The ladies want water," Pedro mocks. "Isn't that right, ladies?"

"Sure," I nod. "Whatever you say, *jefe.*"

Pedro pokes the gun barrel in my gut—a gut that's still sore from the gun butt he jammed in it not too long ago.

"You call me, boss, huh?" he says. "I like it when you call me boss. Let me show you what your boss is capable of, gringo." Raising his weapon, he takes aim at Rodney, fires, hits him square in the chest. Then, turning fast, he grabs Leslie by the head of her hair. He pulls her down to the ground, pulls her T-shirt up and over her breasts, yanking her bra off with it. Stuffing his face into her face, he tries to kiss her.

"Stop, you son of a bitch!" I shout.

That's when Military Man Juan raises up his AK-47, triggers a bullet that whizzes past my head like a hornet.

To the left of me, Rodney is struggling to stay alive, a small geyser of arterial blood pouring forth from the center of his chest. To my right, Military Man Juan is aiming the black barrel of his assault weapon at my head while hungrily watching his partner commit rape. Directly before me, Leslie is on her back, struggling to stave off Pedro's bearded face and hands.

"Give it to her," Juan chants, the smile on his face wide and beaming. "Give it to her and then I give it to her."

Leslie lifts her head, opens her mouth, chomps down on Pedro's bottom lip. The lip explodes in blood. Pedro screams, raises his right hand high, brings it swiftly down, slapping Leslie hard. She lets loose with a high-pitched scream that rattles my bones. Then she spits in his face. Once more raising his right hand while holding her to the jungle floor with his left, he makes a tight fist which he uses to punch her square in the face.

"I'm going to kill you for this!" Leslie shouts.

My heart beating in my throat, I am helpless to do anything about it.

Or am I?

Out the corner of my left eye, I spot Rodney's machete. It's lying in the grass, only a few feet to the left of me. With Pedro entirely occupied and Juan absorbed in the action, it might be possible to shift myself to the left. I don't hesitate to do it. Sliding my booted feet on the damp grass, I inch my way toward the machete. Juan might be aiming the gun at me, but thus far he has no idea what I'm doing. It takes maybe thirty seconds for me to cover the few feet to the blade, but I manage it without drawing the attention of either two bandits.

I drop down onto my belly, reach out, grab hold of the blade's grip.

Juan turns to me.

"Stupid fucking gringo!" he snaps, shouldering his weapon, firing off a burst that hits the ground only a half inch before my head, sending dirt flying up into my face.

Pulling myself up to my knees, I bark, "Leslie!"

Then I toss the blade into the earth directly beside her right hand. As if anticipating my every move, she grabs the machete grip with her right hand, yanks it out of the ground, swings the blade against Pedro's left elbow. The blade impales itself halfway into his arm, causing him to shriek like a monkey while jerking his torso up and off of Leslie. She pulls the blade out of his elbow and swings it again, taking his left hand clean off at the wrist.

Military Man Juan fires at me again, but the bullets shoot wildly into the trees. He makes the mistake of pouncing on Leslie, while a crying and screaming Pedro rolls off of her onto his back, his nub of an arm spurting dark arterial blood like a fire hose. Juan lifts the stock of his rifle and brings it down towards the center of Leslie's forehead. But she manages to shift at precisely the right moment, the butt landing instead into the soft earth.

"Eat this, asshole!" Leslie barks, as she whips the blade across the base of Juan's neck. The blade impales itself into the meat, bone, and cartilage, until the furious Leslie pulls it back out and swings once more, severing his head entirely. Leaning herself up onto her left elbow, she stares down into the still alive face on the amputated head. Juan is trying to speak, his dark eyes bulging and wide and fully aware that he's been decapitated. With a smile on her face, she puckers her lips, and as a final gesture of her disgust for the Tupac revolutionaries, spits in his eyes.

I crab my way over to Leslie.

"Are you hurt?"

"I'm good," she says. "Watch out for asshole number two."

Locking eyes onto Pedro, I see him turn onto his stomach. He's crawling away from us on an empty patch of brown earth. Raising himself up awkwardly onto his feet, he tries to run away. But something stops him dead. He turns to us, his stub gripped in his right hand, the blood still spilling out. It's not hard to see that he is sinking. The area of brown earth he's stepped into isn't stable soil.

It's quicksand.

By the looks of it, clay quicksand, which is not uncommon for this part of the jungle. The look on Pedro's scraggily bearded face is one of horror and shock.

Eyes wide, he pleads, "Help me! Please!"

Leslie turns to me.

"Should we shoot him?"

I glance back at him just as his legs disappear.

"What the hell," I say.

Taking hold of Juan's AK-47, I plant a bead on him. I'm just about to fire a life-ending burst into him when something extraordinary happens. I make out a large commotion in the vegetation as a jaguar jumps out, impaling its fang-filled jaws into Pedro's neck. The rebel's screams are muted as the cat's long teeth enter into his neck, piercing his voice box. The five-foot-long, muscular, black-spots-on-gold-furred cat must have smelled his blood. The cat somehow manages to yank him out of the quicksand without sinking into it herself. The last vision we have of Pedro the revolutionary is of his being dragged off into the brush, his wide black eyes locked onto us the entire way.

Dropping the AK-47, I roll onto my back beside Leslie.

"There's gotta be an easier way of doing book research," I say.

35

There's no time to waste as we pull ourselves back up onto our feet and go to Rodney's aid. But as soon I lay eyes upon him...upon his chest...I can see that he's already gone. The flow of blood coming from the entry wounds in his sternum has abated, all movement ceased, any signs of breathing a historical fact. I take a knee, place my fingers to his jugular, and confirm his death.

Running my open hand gently over his eyes, I close his lids.

I stand.

"It's just you and me now, Leslie," I say. "Still want to go on?"

She's pulling down her shirt and straightening out her hair with both her hands.

"Everyone has been killed but you and me," she says. "We stop now it wouldn't be like giving up on us. It would be like giving up on our team."

I nod.

"I agree and I love you for that." I pause for a moment while glancing up at the treetops and the rays of brilliant sunshine pouring through them. It's as if I'm looking directly into heaven itself. Then, lowering my head, refocusing my gaze on my agent's beautiful face, "Whatever's out there, Leslie...Whatever it is that is protected inside some cave that's been bored of some unknown mountain, it is so important and so precious that men are willing to murder for it."

Leslie exhales, wipes the beaded perspiration from her brow with the back of her hand, a hand still stained with the blood from the savage who tried to rape her. "I'm sure that whatever is out there deep inside this unforgiving jungle is so incredibly priceless that whoever takes possession of it will be wealthy beyond their wildest dreams."

I shake my head.

"It's more than that, Leslie," I say, setting both my hands on her shoulders. "Way more. The Condor is not just a priceless antiquity. If it is a golden aircraft and it's operational…if it actually flies…then we are about to uncover something that's going to pretty much turn the world upside down ."

"But will people believe us? Believe in the Condor? And is it something we should expose to the world? An object that challenges not something as simple as the history of aviation but the fucking foundations of western civilization and its religion. This isn't about an old plane, Chase, it's about God. The existence of this plane will destroy him if we let it." My agent, inhaling, shakes her head. "Just what the hell is it we're about to pull the lid off of?"

"Leslie," I say, raising my eyes back up at the sun, "what we're about to uncover is nothing less than a portal that leads directly to our makers."

"God," she states.

"Maybe God," I say. "Or maybe something else entirely. Something we've been confusing with God for centuries."

Before we move on, I dig through Rodney's pockets, find his wallet and his unsecured cell phone. I look at the face of his cell, and I can see that for as many times as he's called Keogh III there have been no return calls. I search his texts, and I can see it's the same story. Flipping over to his Gmail, the story of one-sided communications repeats itself yet another time.

I store the phone and wallet inside one of my cargo pants pockets.

"Are you going to alert your employer about the recent deaths?" Leslie says, while picking up Rodney's AR-15 from off the ground. "He really should know."

I shake my head. "He's been oddly if not disturbingly out of reach so far. And I'm not sure why."

"One would think he'd be in touch with you every step of the way."

"True that. But there's something about his lack of communication that bothers me more than his simply not returning our calls or texts."

"And that is, Chase?"

"Something tells me that going in search of this ancient aircraft, as out of this world important that it is, is not the walk in the park it was originally made out to be."

"There are Rodney's and Carlos's dead bodies to prove it, not to mention three crucified guides and one badly decapitated revolutionary."

"And that's just a partial list of casualties, which tells you what?"

She places the AR-15 strap over her shoulder.

"I think I know what you're getting at, Chase," she says, her dark eyes wide and unblinking. "This is a suicide mission, isn't it?"

Me, exhaling. "Keogh never had any intention of our returning. He only wanted to use us to confirm that the Golden Condor does indeed exist inside a cave in an uncharted mountain."

"So what the hell shall we do now?"

"We do what we came here to do. We find the plane and then we fly it out of here. After that, you're going to get me paid, per my signed agreement with Peter Keogh the Third."

"Fly it how? Rodney's dead."

"We'll think of something." I smile. "After all, I'm the Man in the Yellow Hat. Now, let's walk."

With me in the lead, we make for the mountain where Peter Keogh II was last seen alive more than three-quarters of a century ago.

36

Luck is on our side.

The thick vegetation that plagued us for miles thins out the closer we come to the base of the mountain. For some inexplicable reason, my mind wanders. Almost like it were yesterday, I can still recall working side by side with my dad. I was the young digger right out of college and he was the seasoned pro who, at that time, was maybe two or three years younger than I am now. His idea of on-the-job training was to toss me behind the sticks of an old yellow Caterpillar backhoe with the order of, "Just do it." Even now I think Nike stole their ad campaign from him.

But my dad's philosophy was a simple one.

Digging wasn't a matter of placing a big shovel into the ground and coming up with a pile of dirt. It was all about the feel, the instinct, the gut you developed over time for making the right moves. Excavating was like sex. One required gentility, passion, and the entire giving over of one's self in order to make the earth move. And there was no better way for that to happen than to simply get digging, and to learn from your mistakes along the way.

In the end, Dad was right. After two or three busted gas lines that nearly blew me up along with them, and four or five severed electrical lines and one or two serious cave-ins, you learn to develop a sixth sense about precisely where your big hard shovel is supposed to go and where it's not meant to go.

Later on, when we put our digging talents to use in the sandhogging/archeological trade, we also developed a gut for knowing the best productive places to dig as opposed to those that would surely turn up empty. You learn to recognize that little voice inside your head that says, "X marks the spot." Right now, as we exit the jungle and come upon the giant rock of a mountain, I hear that voice loud and clear.

"My God in heaven," Leslie whispers.

"He would most definitely have had something to do with this," I say, as I slowly raise my head to take in the entirety of the colossal wall of black stone which stands before me. "He or a race of ancient beings who were not of this earth anyway."

"Maybe God and these so-called ancient beings are one and the same."

"Maybe."

The cliff face must top off at one thousand vertical meters, past the tree line, its summit hidden behind thick gray-white clouds. What's immediately apparent is that the stone face hasn't formed naturally, but like many of the rock carvings on Machu Picchu, have been chiseled out by someone or something. "Stone face" isn't an indiscriminate term, as the cliff has been carved to resemble a man. But not just any man. This man is most certainly wearing a headdress of sorts. Only, not a true headdress. More like a helmet that covers the entire head and face with a glass visor for protection. Projecting from out of the top of the helmet is something that resembles a hose. A hose for transporting oxygen to the helmet, much like an astronaut would require.

The stonework is so precise, I would dare anyone to try and stick their fingernails in between the joints. Old vines and thick growth hang off of the cliff face, while large birds and bats circle around it, shooting in and out of the fog-like mist which drapes much of the mountain.

"Look, Chase," Leslie speaks up. "A staircase."

It takes me a second or two to tear my eyes away from the mammoth face carved into the rock. But when I do, I begin to take notice of the staircase that's also been carved from out of the rock and that appears to corkscrew itself around the entire vine-covered mountain.

"Where do you think it leads?" Leslie questions.

"Only one way to find out."

I approach the stairs with the machete in hand and, after chopping away some of the vegetation which has grown over the first few steps over the years, turn to Leslie.

"Looks like it's been a while since someone climbed this staircase."

"Time's wasting," she says. For the first time since we entered the forest, she smiles. I recognize that smile because I've seen it painted on the faces of dozens of explorers I've met along the way from Cairo to Kathmandu. It means that Leslie is catching the fever. The very special explorer's fever that can only come from the prospect of uncovering a piece of profound ancient history. Something that might even possess the answers to why man lives on earth and why he has evolved the way he has.

"Follow me," I say, taking my first step up into ancient history.

37

The stairs are narrow and slippery both from the damp air and the moss growth that has formed on them over the years. With no banisters to hang onto or guardrail to keep us from falling off the side, the going is slow and precarious to say the least. Each footstep upwards feels as though I were stepping on smooth rock covered in motor oil. As we climb towards the clouds, the air becomes noticeably cooler and damper.

Up ahead a coiled snake occupies one of the stair treads, as if guarding the mountain.

"Leslie," I say, "give me your gun."

"Great," she says, while slowly handing me the AR-15, "more snakes."

As I shove the barrel into the snake's belly, it raises its head and hisses at me, white fangs bared. Shifting the barrel so that it's positioned just beneath the snake's head, I lift it up off the slippery stone and send it flying off the side. A couple of seconds later we hear the distinct thump the heavy snake makes when it collides with the bush below.

I hand the weapon back to Leslie and we proceed with our ascent. We take the climb slowly, planting our feet on treads hewn out of the obsidian rock thousands of years ago by men who had no conception about modern engineering or its mechanical tools. Yet each step could have only been carved by hand by someone who understood complex construction techniques. Methods that some would say could only have come to them from a species far older, far more knowledgeable, and perhaps more powerful than their own.

Soon we emerge through the tree canopy. The hot sun partially penetrates the never still cloud cover so that at one minute, the sky is filled with sunshine and the next, it's covered over entirely by thick, misting clouds. To my right, the vine-covered, black rock drips with damp condensate. To my left, huge dinosaur-like birds navigate the open air above the treetops. A few of the birds appear to be hungry hawks, searching for spider monkeys and jungle rats to fill their bellies.

As we climb, the mountain narrows and the staircase becomes steeper, making the going even slower and more treacherous. After a time, the mouth of the cave comes into view. The mouth of the cave is also the mouth of the human face carved into the rock. Ingenious. As we close in on the cave entrance the sun once more breaks through the clouds and we are exposed to a panoramic view of the rainforest below.

That's when I spot the runway which has been carved out of the thick forest.

"Do you see that, Leslie?" I say, pointing with my left arm and index finger extended. "That opening. It almost looks like a runway."

"What on God's earth would a runway be doing in the middle of this ancient forest?" Leslie poses.

I pull my binoculars out from under my bush jacket, place them to my eyes.

"You're not going to believe this," I say, "but it is a runway." Handing her the binoculars. "Look. To the far left of the landing strip is a plane. A biplane. A De Havilland Tiger Moth, just like the one Keogh Two was flying when he crashed into the trees almost eighty years ago."

She gazes through the binoculars.

"Could it be the same one?"

"The odds are against it being anything else."

"But he must have destroyed it when he crashed it."

"It's possible the natives have somehow reassembled it, and then created a kind of false runway out of the jungle for it. Perhaps something to please the Gods."

"Or something to lure the Gods, or what you and I know as aliens, back to the mountain and what the mountain protects."

She hands back the binoculars.

I shoot her a look. "Very good deduction, Agent. You're learning fast."

"Let's keep going," she says. "Let's see if a far older airplane is stored inside that cave."

We continue climbing, knowing that only one more short revolution around the mountain separates us from the truth about the ancient aliens and a Golden Condor.

38

We come to the top of the stairs.

Before us is the massive cave opening which also doubles as the "mouth" of the carved mountain. The opening is draped in vines, growth, and thick spider webs. There's a strange, sweet-smelling air that's emanating from the cave. The cool, thick air causes the curtain of webs to pulsate, like the sail on a boat continually filling with wind and then losing it.

"Maybe you should go first," Leslie says, that now familiar tension having returned to her voice, "since you're the Man in the Yellow Hat."

"Funny," I say, "I don't feel like I'm wearing a yellow hat."

Something dawns on me then. Reaching into the bottom, left-hand pocket of my bush jacket, I pull out a small device that was sent to me by one of my fans.

"Don't tell me you're going high tech on us, Chase Baker?"

I peel off the device's plastic protector and then, pulling out my smartphone, slide the playing card–sized device onto it as you would a zoom lens for a smartphone. Clicking onto the device's application, I point it at the cave opening, keeping my eyes on the digital screen.

"This is an infrared thermal camera sensor," I explain. "If there's something alive and moving in there, this thing will pick it up. In theory at least."

"Have you tried it before?"

"I went as far as downloading the application. But then I backed off and forgot about it."

"You're not comfortable with the digital age."

I cock my head. "I envy Keogh Two, flying here in a biplane, searching for a trail using only his eyes."

"You told me he used a camera. High tech for his time."

"I suppose," I say, bobbing the device in my hand. "But stuff like this takes the fun out of exploration."

"It also decreases the chances of spontaneous attack from a dangerous predator. You should have thought about using it back there in the jungle. We might have avoided the ambush from the hostiles and the Tupac revolutionaries."

I shake my head. "The jungle is too massive, too filled with life of every variety. The sensors would have gone ballistic. It only works in enclosed spaces."

"Well, Chase, let's put it to work."

Once more aiming the device at the cave, I look for a sign of life. At first, nothing appears, but then suddenly, several small blips fly across the screen.

"Bats," I say. "I'll bet the mortgage those are bats."

"Or spiders scurrying across those webs."

"That too is a possibility, if not a probability. This is a cave after all."

I continue with the examination, looking for something big to appear for me in a radiant green glow. I'm just about to replace the device and the phone back into my pocket on my bush jacket when something appears and at the same time, causes my heart to skip a beat.

"You have got to be kidding me," I whisper, my pulse picking up.

"What is it?" Leslie says, trying to get a look over my shoulder without losing her footing on the slippery step.

Locking my eyes onto the screen, I see what is undoubtedly a bipedal creature that's walking around inside the cave.

"It's a man, Leslie," I say. "Most definitely a man."

39

"How can you be certain it's a man?" Leslie says. "What if it's a monkey? Or a gorilla?"

"Gorillas don't exist here," I say. "And if memory serves me well, the largest monkey in the Amazon is a howler monkey and they're only about a foot and a half to two feet tall. Whatever or whoever this thing is, it is walking like a man. Upright and graceful."

"Hostile natives?" she poses.

"Could be," I say. "In any case, let's be on guard for whatever greets us on the other side of that opening."

Drawing my .45, I thumb off the safety. Then, pulling my LED lamp off my belt, I flick it on and take the first step toward the cave opening. With Leslie close on my tail, I reach out with the pistol barrel and break through the curtain of webs.

"Watch your step, Les. There are vines underfoot. Stay close."

"I'm so close I can feel your heart beating."

The round, high-intensity lamp cuts through a darkness so black it feels like it's possible to pull chunks of the stuff away with my hands. As we move in toward the heart of the cave, the air begins to warm and the once sweet smell gives way to something else. The odor of burning oil.

I stop.

"What's wrong?"

My gut speaks to me, tells me that despite the darkness, we're being monitored by more than one set of eyes.

"We're not alone," I say, my voice a hoarse whisper.

Raising up my .45, I thumb back the hammer.

That's when the solid rock beneath our feet gives way.

40

We're falling rapidly, sliding on our backsides down a slide made of extraordinarily smooth stone. The steeply angled marble ramp banks and curves at sudden angles and it's all I can do to hang on to both the LED flashlight and the pistol. Leslie is screaming, but at the same time, laughing, like she's getting a rush from an amusement park ride.

Then suddenly, we come to the end of the ramp by shooting out of a square-shaped opening positioned at ground level in the wall. We land softly on our backsides onto a stone floor, the momentum causing us to slide for maybe an additional five or six feet.

When I'm able to get my bearings, I shoot Leslie a look. "You okay, Les?"

But she doesn't look at me. Her eyes are fixated on something dead ahead.

"You were right," she says. "We are most definitely not alone."

41

The room is lit with burning torches that are suspended from stone walls that have been carved and polished as smooth as the stone floor and the ceiling overhead. Surrounding us on all sides are natives of the Amazon. They are dressed not only in leather thongs, but also what appears to be a ceremonial costuming. Feathery headdresses and necklaces of shrunken heads, along with bracelets of bone and teeth. They point spears at us and stare into our faces with dark-eyed gazes.

"If this were a situation straight out of one of my slush pile novels," Leslie says under her breath, "it would be the part where we say, 'We come in peace.'"

Uncocking the .45, I then slowly set it onto the stone floor. Then I do the same with the flashlight. Holding up both my hands as if in surrender, I begin to rise up onto my feet. Acting in unison, the natives move in closer while cocking back the arms that support the spears, as if about to thrust the deadly weapons into our chests.

I stand anyway and smile.

"My name is Chase," I say, knowing that more than likely they will have no idea what I'm saying. But it's the tone of my voice that counts. "This is my associate, Leslie."

More staring, more aiming of the spears.

"Perhaps you can tell me who's in charge?" I say in as gentle a tone as possible, while maintaining my smile.

That's when I hear footsteps coming from way off at the other end of the long rectangular room. Not bare feet on stone, but actual leather soles click-clacking on the stone.

"Stand back," I hear a man speak in English. American English. "Please get back, all of you."

The band of natives splits in half, making two neat rows of warrior men who now face one another in the great polished stone room. They also make room for someone who, according to the laws of nature and God, should not now be staring me in the face.

A man by the name of Peter Keogh II.

42

He's dressed like he's about to take flight in the De Havilland Tiger Moth parked out on the strip carved out of the jungle. A worn leather coat over khaki or canvas pants which are stuffed inside knee-length lace-up leather boots. Army-style work shirt, the chest pocket stuffed to the button's breaking points. He wears a leather holster which holds a Colt Peacemaker on his right-hand hip, and on his head, a leather flight hat, a pair of goggles pulled up high on his forehead. He's sporting a thin and trimmed mustache on his upper lip, a la Errol Flynn, while brown leather gloves cover his hands.

"Quite the ride down here, ain't it?" he says, not without a pleasant smile.

He holds out his right hand.

"Peter Keogh the Second," he says in a boisterous but welcoming tone. "Damned glad to meet ya."

I hesitate at first, because I can't believe what I'm looking at. It's the year 2014. By all accounts, this man disappeared from the world when his plane crashed into the trees back in 1939 when he was forty-something years old. That would put him well over a hundred. Judging by the gray in his mustache and the strands of salt and pepper hair that stick out from under his flight cap, I wouldn't peg him for anything older than fifty or fifty-five. But how can that be?

Leslie leans into me.

"Are we dead? Or are we dreaming this?"

"Relax," I say out the corner of my mouth. "Just keep thinking about what a great book this is going to make."

"Better be fiction, because no one is ever going to believe this shit."

I turn back to Keogh II.

"Mr. Keogh," I say.

"Call me Pete," he says. "All my friends do. Isn't that right, Amma?" He turns to one of the natives, who nods while maintaining his sour, I-want-to-stab-the-gringos-with-my-spear expression. "Oh well, Amma is a sour puss," Keogh adds with a giggle. "You know anything about the Tupi tribes, Mister ahhhh, Mister ..."

"I'm Chase," I say, taking hold of his leather-gloved hand, gripping it tightly. "Chase Baker." Nodding toward Leslie. "This is Leslie. My partner."

He peels away his hand, removes the glove. Then, taking a step forward, he takes hold of Leslie's hand while gallantly dropping down onto one knee. Bringing the back of Leslie's hand to his face, he plants a kiss on it.

"Leslie," he says. "I am enchanted to know thee."

Leslie beams, her face turning red.

"Oh my," she says, "a real gentleman."

Releasing her hand, he stands, nods.

"Why thank you. Mom and Pop taught me well." Then, biting down on his bottom lip, "Say, you wouldn't happen to have a cigarette, would you? A Lucky Strike or a Chesterfield maybe. "

As if on instinct I pat my pockets.

"I quit some years ago," I confess.

He smirks.

"Seems I've quit as well. But not by choice. Cigarette girls are hard to come by down here. Like Tommy Dorsey records."

He smiles, like he's having a ball.

"Mr. Keogh—"

"Pete."

"Yes, Pete. Do you have any idea how old you are?"

He laughs like a boy.

"Well, last I checked," he says. "Forty-two."

"Forty-two," I repeat like a question.

"Give or take a few decades. You see, Chase, it's hard to keep track in my line of work."

"Your line of work." Another question.

"You see," he says, "I'm a pilot."

"So we've heard," Leslie jumps in. "We came down here to look for you, amongst other things."

He nods. "And I have always known that you or someone like you would eventually come knocking on my stone front door. It was just a matter of time. Now here you are." Crossing his arms over his chest. "But if you don't mind, can you tell me who sent you?"

"Your son," I say.

He smiles.

"My son? My God, I have a son whom I haven't seen in forever." He takes a step back, sets both hands on his hips while assuming a facial expression that sings of shock, wonderment, and curiosity. "Tell me, what's my son like now?"

I press my lips together.

"I'm afraid he's a bit sick these days."

"Oh no," he says, eyes wide, as if I'm talking about a boy of five or six years old. "Cold? Influenza?"

"Worse than that, I'm afraid. Your son has cancer, Pete."

His face goes pale. "A child should never be stricken with cancer."

"Your son is seventy-five years old, Peter," I say. "He's older than his father."

"But how can that be? Has time escaped me entirely? Do you know I knew him as a newborn baby?" His eyes are blinking rapidly, and he gives his head a shake as if it helps get a grip on the bizarre reality he's now been faced with.

Just then, more footsteps come from behind Keogh. Booted feet. Not the bare feet of the natives.

"Who's that?" I say to Keogh, crouching down and retrieving my .45 while Leslie cautiously picks up the AR-15.

He looks at me wide-eyed.

"I have no idea. I should be the only westerner down here, next to you two."

"All that changes right now," comes the voice of a man.

As he comes closer, I am able to make out the man's face, and his identity shocks me almost as much as Keogh II's did.

"Peter Keogh the Second," I say as he approaches, "please meet Mister Peter Keogh the Third. Your son."

43

Keogh III locks his gaze upon his maker. I can tell he's trying his best to work up something to say to a man who not only gave him life so long ago, but who should also be long dead by now. But instead of making words, all he can manage is to open and close his mouth while his Adam's apple bobs up and down inside his thin, if not sickly, pale neck.

At the same time, Keogh II eyes his long-lost son like a young father who is getting his first real peek at his newborn baby. The old pilot holds out his arms as if to bear hug his aged and dying boy.

"Behold your father, son," he says.

But something very strange happens then. Keogh III doesn't step forward, enter into his dad's loving arms. Instead, he takes a deliberate step backwards. And then another, just to prove he meant the first one.

"I don't know if you're real," he says with a shake of his head, "or if you're someone's idea of a joke. But whatever you are, I don't want you touching me. Got it?"

"Son," Keogh II says, his voice suddenly painfully hoarse, his smile now turned upside down, "why do you speak to me this way?"

Keogh III exhales, bites down hard on his bottom lip. His face is pale, and so gaunt it almost hurts to look at it. "If you're real…If you are genuinely my father and not some crazy imposter who's followed me down here in order to confuse me and sabotage my mission, then what I want to ask you is this: Did it ever occur to you to maybe find a phone and give me a call at some point over the past seventy-five years?"

"Son," the old flier says, "there are no phones down here. There's no real time to speak of. How was I to know that you have grown up, and aged as much as you have?"

"You would have known had you attempted to contact me."

"Look at me, son. You're right. In many ways, I'm not real. Since crashing into the jungle, I've been given a special gift. And it's something you would never understand."

The cancer-ridden Keogh nods. "I'll just have to take your word for it, old man." Then, turning to me, "Enough of this useless chatter. Time to get down to business."

Keogh III is accompanied by two men dressed entirely in black. They wear jungle boots, cargo pants, and work shirts with the Keogh Enterprises logo sewn into the chest pocket over the heart. The logo comes in the shape of an old DC-11 propeller driven cargo plane from the 1930s and 40s. They're both holding black Heckler and Koch HK416 automatic weapons, the barrels of which are aimed precariously at us.

"I'll give you this much, Mr. Baker," Keogh III says, "you are positively dripping with tenacity."

"What a surprise to see you too, boss," I say. "Thanks for answering our calls."

Keogh III maintains a tightlipped, pale face. He's wearing an olive green bush jacket and matching pants, both of which are soaked through. The clothing swims on his sickly, near skeletal-like frame. For footwear, he's sporting the identical black jungle boots as his men. His black and gray baseball cap sports the same Keogh Enterprises logo as the shirts, only larger and more colorful.

"Frankly, Mr. Baker," he says, his voice hardly more than a whisper, "I didn't expect you to live long enough for me to ever speak to you again."

Leslie takes a step forward, nudges me in the bicep.

"It was him all along," she says. "He's the son of a bitch who set us up. He was his own mole. The mole that Pedro spoke about."

"Yes," I say, staring at the rifle barrels. "But why? Why send us on this mission only to kill us off in the process?"

"Because I wanted you to confirm for me what this crazy bastard couldn't confirm," Keogh III says, his eyes poised on his father. "That a trail did indeed exist in the jungle and that it would lead me to this cave in the mountain. Once that was done, I'd have no use for you."

"Who you calling crazy bastard?" Keogh II barks, his eyes once more filling with tears. "That's no way to speak to your father."

The old pilot approaches his even older son once more, again opening up his arms for a hug. Now that they're standing so close, the family resemblance is uncanny.

"Back off, old man," Keogh III insists. Then, holding his bare hand out to me, "I'll be glad to relieve you of your weapon, Chase."

Exhaling, I place it in his palm. Then, his eyes on Leslie, "You too," he says.

She surrenders her AR-15.

"Peter Junior," Keogh II says, "don't you want to hug your father?"

"In case you haven't noticed, old man," the younger Keogh says, "I'm dying. I'm also thirty-plus years older than you right now. But you are going to reverse that for me."

"Son," Keogh II says, bearing the frown of the truly confused, "I don't understand."

"You are in the possession of the most coveted archaeological prize known to man," Keogh III says. "The Golden Condor. The very aircraft or, should I say, spacecraft, that was flown here by ancient aliens from another solar system. It's here in this cave. I want it for two reasons."

"And those reasons are?" I chime in.

"That aircraft is going to save my life," he says. "And then it's going to make me the wealthiest man in the world."

"You are out of your mind, son," the old pilot says. "You have been stricken not only with a cancer but with a sickness that's far worse." Crossing his arms over his chest. "Greed."

"Shut the hell up, old man."

Keogh II's eyes suddenly lose their teary sadness and instead become the eyes of an angry man.

"You watch your tone, sonny boy," he grouses, lowering his

arms.

If things aren't bizarre enough, I'm watching a forty-two-year-old father scold his seventy-five-year-old son.

"Marcus," Keogh III says.

Immediately, the goon standing over my employer's right shoulder shifts himself so that he's facing the line of shoulder-to-shoulder natives to my right.

"Patrick," Keogh III adds.

That's when the second goon positions himself so that he's facing the line of natives on my left.

"Proceed!" Keogh III orders.

Shouldering their weapons, the goons commit mass murder.

44

It takes only a matter of seconds for the slaughter to be completed. Afterwards, the goons change out their clips and stand at attention, awaiting new orders.

Keogh II's face goes pale under his leather flight cap. He eyes the death and destruction all around him, the blood pooling on the stone floor as the members of the ancient Tupi tribe bleed out.

"You will be sorry for this," he whispers angrily to his offspring. "You are not my son. No son of mine would commit a sin like this."

"Save it for later, Dad," Keogh III says. "For now, I want you to lead me to the Condor. You are going to pilot that plane to a place that will save my life and make me young again, just like you, my father, my maker."

"And if I refuse?"

"You won't refuse. Trust me."

"And how is that, sonny?"

"Marcus," Keogh III says again.

That's when the goon cocks his weapon once more, aims it at Leslie, and fires.

The single shot hits her in the stomach.

Leslie collapses to the floor like sack of rags and bones.

I drop to my knees, press both my hands against her wound. But the blood is gushing out from between my fingers.

"You evil son of a bitch!" I shout. "I will kill you for this."

"I'm going to die anyway, Chase. And so is your lovely Leslie. That is unless dear old dad here leads us to the Golden Condor."

I press my hand against Leslie's jugular. She's alive, but the pulse is fading fast.

"You hang in there, Les," I say. "I'm gonna get you help."

She looks up at me with wide eyes. She's in too much pain and shock to talk.

"You see, Chase," Keogh III says, "you and me have the same problem now. If we don't get to that aircraft immediately, we both lose something we can never get back."

I look up at the old pilot.

"Peter," I say. "You gotta help us."

That's when I see him feeling for the six gun that's been hidden until now by his leather aviator's coat.

"Now now, Dad," Keogh III says. "Old men of one hundred fifteen shouldn't be playing with guns."

Keogh III reaches for the gun, snatches it out of his father's holster.

"Genuine relic," he says, shoving the barrel into his pant waist.

Keogh II nods, exhales as though shamed to have been robbed of his weapon so easily.

"Follow me," he says in a dejected tone. "The aircraft is docked overhead."

45

While I cradle the bleeding Leslie in my arms, the two goons follow close behind, their weapons poised on our backs. Keogh II leads us up a set of narrow stone stairs to another room, this one far wider and longer than the one below it. But like the first smaller room, this area too is illuminated in the golden glow of wall-mounted firelit torches.

Positioned in the very center of the room is a sight like I have never before witnessed.

The plane is at least as large as a modern fighter jet, only its skin isn't metallic, but instead, golden, as if constructed of solid gold sheets. The wings are short, but swept, while the back stabilizer is shaped like a V. There seems to be one power source of an engine which is mounted to the very top of the fuselage directly over a cockpit that resembles a bird's beak.

A condor's beak.

There's no landing gear to speak of. Instead the aircraft simply hovers ten feet above the stone floor. It's one of the most remarkable objects I have ever witnessed.

"Come this way, everyone," Keogh II encourages us to follow.

I trail close behind, Leslie bleeding so badly, the blood is pouring onto the floor.

When Keogh II positions himself directly under the belly of the craft, he turns to me and orders me to stay where I am. What he has to do now, he must do by himself.

Standing straight and stiff, his arms held tightly against his sides, he positions his face upwards, so that he's gazing up at the underside of the craft. That's when two beams of bright laser light shoot down, striking both his eyes. He wobbles for a second or two until the laser lights cease. A loud metal against metal bang occurs then, which reverberates throughout the room, and the plane's underbelly begins to open up, the bottom hatch lowering itself down onto the stone so that it provides us with a ramp for entering into her.

"Now," Keogh II says. "This way."

I go to him and carry Leslie up into the craft.

There's nothing inside the Condor that resembles an airplane.

No seats, no doors, no porthole windows for gazing outside the craft. The low-ceilinged metallic tube contains only several floor-mounted tables that are made of metal, or something like metal. I lay Leslie on one of these tables while the rest of the men enter into the area behind me.

"Everyone lies down on one of the tables," Keogh II insists.

"What about you?" his son asks.

Keogh II taps a bare wall with his index finger as if a panel of buttons exists there, and an invisible door slides open.

"I'm flying," he says.

Positioning himself down into a cockpit-like chair, an assemblage of pedals, levers, and periscope-like viewfinders slowly emerge from out of nowhere and mold to his exact physical specifications. I am reminded of the familiar stone carving of the ancient Incan pilot who appeared to be flying a craft outfitted with identical instruments and controls. For decades scientists have been trying to explain that carving. Now an explanation is finally at hand.

The hatch closes and the craft goes pitch dark.

"What now?" I say.

"Just close your eyes," Keogh II insists.

I close my eyes and a strange sensation emanates up from the steel table. It's a kind of electrical charge that doesn't paralyze me, but instead holds me in place like a half dozen invisible thick leather belts and straps have been wrapped around me and buckled secure. Even my pulse and heartbeat seem to be slowing so that I suddenly feel like I'm not entirely awake, as though by lying back on this hard table, I have somehow automatically entered into a dream-state.

A loud thunder follows and then a clockwise circling movement occurs. I open my eyes to sneak a look into the cockpit, and that's when I see that the two metallic sheets or shields that were covering the windshield have been lowered. Keogh II punches something and we begin heading in the direction of a stone wall, until the stone wall rapidly lowers and like a rocket we shoot beyond the cave and the mountain.

"This is it, people," the old flier barks, his voice resonating in my head.

Those are the last words I remember hearing before he punches something else, and I pass out from excessive forces of gravity.

46

I can't tell if what I am seeing and experiencing is a vivid dream or reality.

I'm floating above the earth, my body entirely suspended in space. The aircraft is no longer there. It's as if I have been ejected from it and now float helplessly in outer space with no means to control whether I will live or die. Curiously I am not afraid. In fact, I feel empowered, not like I'm about to drift away into an endless black space, but instead have come face to face with heaven.

Then I see Leslie.

She is far off in the distance, but coming closer to me all the time. That gunshot wound is still visible, the entry wound in her stomach dripping dark red blood. But the closer she comes to me, the smaller the wound gets, the more the blood disappears. By the time she reaches me, the wound has disappeared entirely.

She smiles and takes hold of my hands.

"It's okay," she says. "I'm not in pain anymore."

Releasing my hands, she turns and leaves me, drifting away from me like a long-haired angel until she disappears entirely from view.

The dream shifts…

Suddenly I am on my back on one of the steel tables. I am not alone. To my left, Peter Keogh III is also situated on his back on a steel table. To my right, the Keogh Enterprises goons are also lying on their backs on two separate tables, their eyes closed. They seem to be fast asleep, their weapons still gripped in their hands.

I try and lift myself off the table, but I can't. I'm paralyzed from head to toe. I can see, hear, feel. But I can't move. Shifting my eyes to my feet, I see Keogh II standing along with three figures who are shorter and thinner than him. They appear human but not entirely. They are dressed in gray clothing that fits tightly to their skin and their heads are shaved. Their movements are slow and deliberate, but not threatening. I hear voices, but I cannot possibly make out the language being spoken. The conversation, however, seems to be a pleasant one.

As the conversation comes to an end, the three small figures approach Keogh III. They hold their hands over him for a time while his body enters into convulsions.

The dream shifts once more…

I feel myself flying again. Dropping out of the sky like an asteroid. It's so hot I am breaking out in a sweat, but not so hot that I burn. Struggling to look up from the table, I can see that the interior skin of this aircraft glows bright orange. Something goes bang, like we've just broken through some kind of barrier, and just like that the orange glow disappears.

I close my eyes and drift away.

Moments later, when I come to, I find myself seated up against the stone wall where the Golden Condor is once more parked. Keogh II stands in front of the two goons who are holding their guns on him. Set before the old pilot is a gurney. I can see that there's a body set out on it with a white sheet laid over it. My heart sinks then, because I know who the body belongs to.

Leslie.

Standing off to the side, looking at his reflection in a square piece of hand-held mirror, is Peter Keogh III.

"Fantastic," he says. "Truly fantastic."

From where I'm seated I can see how much he's changed since having visited the heavens in the Golden Condor. His once pale skin has returned to its youthful tanned tone. His thin patches of gray-white hair have now given over to a rich thick head of blond curls. His eyes are alive and blue while his body appears to be muscular and agile. The body of a man in his mid-twenties.

He tosses the mirror to the floor, where it shatters. Looking down at it, I see the faces of the two Keoghs multiplied one hundred times in the jagged broken pieces of mirror glass.

"You did good, Dad," Keogh III says. "I'm sorry it didn't work out for the girl. A damned shame really."

"Please don't refer to me as your dad," Keogh II says. "I did what you asked me to do, now go in peace so that Chase and I might see to it that this young lady has a proper burial."

"Boys," Peter Keogh III barks.

The goons shoulder their weapons, both barrels aimed point-blank for the old pilot's leather-capped head.

"We're not leaving this place without the Golden Condor. That means we need you to do a little more flying."

"You must be mad," the old pilot says. "That aircraft belongs to the Incan people. Before that it belonged to the universe. One day it will belong to the universe again."

"Now it belongs to me."

"For your prized collection?" I say, from where I'm seated against the wall.

I pull myself back up onto my two feet and stand, a bit out of balance.

"Yes, for my prized collection. But that's the least of it." He waves his hand in the direction of the Golden Condor. "This isn't just a plane. It's history and it's the future, and it's proof that we are not alone. It will make me the most influential man on the planet and perhaps beyond the planet."

"Your father is right," I say. "You're quite mad."

"And you're about to be quite dead, Mr. Baker," he says. "Boys, take care of him."

The goons turn at me, the two black barrels on their weapons staring me in the face like twin devils.

47

But something happens then.

In the split second before the goons depress their fingers on the triggers of their automatic rifles, Keogh II shouts out, "Chase, get down!"

He drops down onto his chest and I do the same. That's when three bright beams of laser light shoot forth from the belly of the Golden Condor, the brilliant beams connecting directly with the heads of the goons and Peter Keogh III. The men fall to the stone floor on their backs. They seem paralyzed, until they begin to writhe in convulsions, white foam spurting from their mouths. As fast and as sudden as the light shoots out of the craft, it then disappears.

Sucking in a breath, I quickly grab their weapons, tossing them aside. I also pull the old pilot's six gun from his son's pant waist.

"What the hell was that?" I ask Keogh II, as I hand him back his Colt Peacemaker.

"In the time since I've been down here, I believe a very famous British pop group sang a hit tune called, 'With a Little Help from My Friends.' Well, that, my adventurous amigo, was a little help from my friends."

"Your friends up there, you mean," I say, now knowing that the small men I saw communicating with the old pilot up in the spacecraft was not a dream, but a dream-like reality.

I look down at the goons. They are no longer writhing or moving. They are clearly dead. My eyes shift to my employer. He too is lying on his back, perfectly still, his young face no longer full of life, but having taken on the chalk white pallor of the newly departed.

Looking into Keogh II's eyes I can see that he is not taking the sudden death of his long-lost son lightly. His eyes fill, as a tear runs down his cheek. He lowers himself onto one knee, placing his brown gloved hand on his son's chest.

"I'm sorry, son," he says. "But you left me no choice."

With his father's hand laid upon his sternum, Peter Keogh III's face begins to change. The youthful skin begins to dry up, becoming wrinkled and saggy. The thick blond curls fall out, until all that's visible is a bald scalp tattooed with age spots. The muscular body loses its tone, the musculature turning to worn-out flesh. Not only has death touched Peter Keogh III, but so has advanced old age. His final punishment for the murders he's committed and the murder he would inevitably commit in the name of his own fortune and glory. How damned tragic that it had to come from his own father. Or perhaps, in the end, entirely fitting.

Keogh II makes the sign of the cross and stands. He goes to Leslie, pulls the sheet off her face. Even in death, her face is as beautiful and perfect as ever. It makes my throat close in on itself just to look at her.

"I want you to do something for me," the old pilot says.

"What is it?" I say, my voice cracking.

"I want you to turn around."

I nod and do it.

I begin to feel an earthquake-like shaking and a rattling that's so violent, it's like the entire mountain is about to collapse in on the interior stone structures. The trembling is accompanied by a bright light that's different from the lasers that sucked the life from Peter Keogh III and his goons. This light is more like the morning sun shining through an opening in the treetops. I feel it's warmth on my back, and I swear to you now, I can feel it throughout my own body, like a newborn child can feel the heart beating in his mother's chest the first time she holds him tightly.

Then, as the light slowly fades, the mountain goes still.

My body feels soaked with sweat and my eyes are filled with

tears, and I can't exactly explain why, other than knowing that what just happened inside that big ancient stone room is nothing short of miraculous.

"You can turn around now," Keogh II says.

And when I do, I know that I was absolutely right. What I'm witnessing is nothing short of a miracle.

She's sitting up on the table.

Leslie, her eyes wide and blinking, the life returned to her flesh and blood, her long dark hair draping her face like an angel.

"I must have fallen asleep," she says. "Are we in space?"

"No, Les," I say, trying my best to hold back my tears, "we're back on the solid ground."

"What happened?" she asks. Then, while looking deeply into my eyes, "Why are you crying?"

Keogh II smiles, adjusts the leather cap on his head and the goggles that rest on his forehead.

"Think I'll tend to something downstairs," he says. "You two take all the time you need."

He leaves.

Leaning down, I rest my head on Leslie's now healed chest, and cry my eyes out.

48

Two days later, Leslie and I are doing something we never would have guessed just five days ago when this whole adventure began. We are boarding a single-engine biplane that was constructed back before my parents were born. Keogh II hops into the cockpit directly behind us, pulls the goggles down over his eyes. He's wearing a white silk scarf which he's wrapped around his neck, and he's smiling proudly.

"Been a long time since I fired up the Tiger Moth," he says. "This really should be quite the treat."

"How long exactly?" Leslie says, as she takes hold of my hand inside the cramped leather covered seat we're sharing.

He takes a minute to think about it while scratching at the scruff under his chin with his thumb and index finger, his eyes peering up at the hot sun that shines down on this landing strip in the jungle.

Lowers his eyes and catching both our gazes, he says, "Why seventy-five years to be exact."

"Seventy-five years," I say. "You mean you never thought even once about flying yourself out of this jungle back to civilization?"

"Oh sure, I thought about it. Thought about it a lot. But the plane has always been inoperable. Until a couple of days ago when I was able to make a special request of some friends who reside in, let's call it, a higher place."

"God," Leslie whispers into my ear.

"Let's just go with it," I whisper back, recalling the little men who were conversing with Keogh II while the Golden Condor was still racing through space.

"Now make yourselves comfortable," the old pilot barks. "And remember to hold on."

A portly white man who's dressed in baggy grease-stained overalls and wearing a baseball hat with the logo of the old Brooklyn Dodgers appears suddenly as if from out of nowhere. He's wiping his hands with an old oily rag. Pocketing the rag, he takes hold of the old wood prop with both his thick hands.

"Switch on," shouts the old pilot. "Contact!"

"Roger that," says the mechanic. "Have a swell trip. Bring me back a newspaper. I wanna catch up on the Brooklyn Dodgers."

"Sure we know what we're doing?" Leslie says to me, her eyes front. "Why do I get the feeling we're about to be flown out of the Amazon rainforest in a ghost plane being piloted by a ghost pilot who works with a ghost mechanic who still thinks the Dodgers play baseball in Brooklyn?"

"Maybe we're all ghosts and just don't know it," I say. "In which case, we can't possibly die because we're already dead."

The propeller catches and the engine roars to life, its pistons spitting excess fuel and acrid smoke.

"Hang on," the old pilot announces. "Here we go!"

The plane inches forward until it comes to a slow roll. Then, picking up speed, it's trembling body cruises along the landing strip, the engine roaring and straining until just like that, we feel a jolt and we're airborne, our wheels barely clearing the tops of the trees. The plane bounces and bucks for a few moments, and I feel my stomach rise up into my throat while the old pilot circles the runway. Looking out over the side, I see the portly mechanic looking up at us. He's bearing a broad grin, and waving at us with his grease towel. When he lowers his hand finally, he begins walking back toward the tree-line. But before he gets there, he disappears, like a piece of tissue paper suddenly lit up by flame.

"Okay now!" Keogh II, barks as the biplane levels off, "I'm gonna open the old bird up!"

The old pilot lets loose with a hoot and a holler as the engine roars and we head on into the newly rising sun of a brand new day.

EPILOGUE

New York City
Two Weeks Later

I'm lying on the couch inside Leslie's new agency office, which is located on the fourth floor of a newly renovated prewar building on downtown Broadway. I've got a tennis ball in my hand and I'm playing pitch and catch with the exposed brick wall in front of me.

Leslie is sitting behind her new glass and steel desk. She's reading the morning paper while sipping a cup of coffee and picking at a bagel with her fingertips.

"Says here the bodies of financier and avid airplane collector Peter Keogh the Third was uncovered inside the ruins of an ancient Incan settlement which had been built into a mountain in the Amazon jungle not five miles from Machu Picchu. The ruins are reported not having been touched by human hands in nearly a thousand years. The entry had to be blasted in order to get at the bodies. The only way they were located at all is by their cell phones, which gave away their positions via GPS. Sources are still trying to figure out how the men were able to enter into the ruins in the first place."

I toss the ball against the wall, catch it.

"Guess we'll never know," I say.

I hear her put the paper down.

"Chase," she says, "how come you never told me exactly what happened to me up in the aircraft?"

"What's to tell? We went for a ride and you passed out. End of story."

"But you saw something up there, didn't you? What did you see?"

I toss the ball again. Catch it again.

"I don't know. Stuff."

"What stuff?"

More pitch and catch.

"Let's just say that maybe, just maybe, there is such a thing as ancient aliens and that those ancient aliens might be more like God than we know. Or vice versa, of course."

"So what you're saying is God and ancient aliens are one and the same."

"What's so hard to believe about that? God rides around in a chariot of fire while accompanied by a bunch of flying angels. Maybe they helped out ancient man for a while. Taught him some things. Like flight, for instance. That knowledge got lost over time until the Wright bros came along and rediscovered it."

She lets that one settle for a minute, picks off a tiny piece of bagel, slips it into her mouth.

"How come the ruins we witnessed were in perfect condition? How come whoever entered into them to recover Keogh the Third didn't spot the aircraft?"

"The old pilot must have known they were coming and took off for greener pastures. So to speak. Maybe he destroyed the joint just to make it look good."

"Destroyed the place," she repeats. "You think he was a real man? A real man who was one hundred fifteen years old yet looked not a day over fifty?"

I look at her over my shoulder.

"Up there in the sky," I say. "Way up in the far reaches of the universe ... that's where you'll find the answers."

"You mean I'll find out how I was cured of a mortal bullet wound in a matter of moments."

"Among other things."

"Keogh the Second was one of them, wasn't he?"

"One of what?"

"Not sure I can get myself to say it, so I'll just say it anyway...Aliens. Ancient or otherwise. So was the grease monkey who thought the Dodgers still live in Brooklyn."

"He flew us to Cuzco in a biplane, didn't he? That sound like a little gray man in a flying saucer to you?"

"He dropped us off in an empty field and told us to walk the rest of the three miles on foot when there is a perfectly good airport in Cuzco. And did you notice that when he took back off, the plane didn't seem to fade into the horizon, it sort of suddenly vanished into thin air?"

"Optical illusion," I say, shrugging my shoulders.

"You love this, don't you?"

"Love what?"

"Being cryptic."

"I like saving the juicy bits for my new novel."

"Speaking of which, when do I get to see a first draft? I got bills coming in now that the agency is back in action."

"Soon. I'll be done in a month. It's called *Chase Baker and the Golden Condor*. Whaddya think?"

"I like it." Then, "When are you meeting your daughter?"

"We're doing dinner at the pizza joint downstairs from my apartment. You wanna join us? Or are you meeting back up with the gynie?"

"The gynie is long gone-baby-gone."

I turn to her. "Me likey."

I listen to her get up from her chair, come around her desk. I bounce the ball off the wall once more, but this time, she snatches it up. Making her way to the office door, she opens it just a tiny bit.

"Hold my calls until further notice," she says through the narrow opening. "And girls, no listening through the door."

I hear the door close behind her, the lock engaged.

My literary agent comes back to the couch, sets herself down on the edge, her skirt riding up high enough on her thighs to show some serious smooth skin.

"Wanna play breach-the-professional-relationship-between-author-and-agent?" She smiles.

"Okay, you play the hot cougar agent, and I'll play the struggling young author who just can't seem to get a break."

She leans into me while undoing the top button on her blouse.

"Oh, I sooo love your writing, Mr. Baker," she says in her best imitation Marilyn Monroe. "It makes me sooo hot."

"You're hired," I say, wrapping my arms around her, pulling her into me.

"I'll have my people draw up contracts right away," she whispers before kissing my lips softly, passionately.

Outside the window, a fire truck speeds past, its sirens piercing the old brick walls of the new Leslie Singer Literary Agency building. By the looks of it, this isn't the only joint that's on fire in New York City.

THE END

ABOUT THE AUTHOR

Vincent Zandri is the *New York Times* and *USA Today* best-selling author of more than sixteen novels, including *The Innocent, Godchild, The Remains, Moonlight Falls,* and *The Shroud Key.* A freelance photojournalist and traveler, he is also the author of the blog *The Vincent Zandri Vox.* He lives in New York and Florence, Italy. For more, go to www.vincentzandri.com.

CPSIA information can be obtained
at www.ICGtesting.com
Printed in the USA
BVOW09s1028110318
510277BV00001B/28/P